The Red Tin Roof

The
Red Tin Roof

Nirmal Verma

Translated from Hindi by
Kuldip Singh

RAVI DAYAL Publisher
Delhi

Published by
RAVI DAYAL Publisher
51 E Sujan Singh Park
New Delhi 110003

Distributed by
ORIENT LONGMAN LTD
Bangalore   Bhubaneshwar   Calcutta   Chennai
Ernakulam   Guwahati   Hyderabad   Lucknow
Mumbai   New Delhi   Patna

ISBN 81 7530 012 4

Typeset by Resodyn, New Delhi 110070
Printed at Pauls Press, New Delhi 110020

For Putul

Part One

In One Breath

Prologue

Everything was ready: the hold-all, bundles, and a suitcase. A coolie stood on the street holding the reins of a pony. The coolie looked indifferently at the house. Four people stood in the sun-splashed passage: a man, a dwarf-like woman — short and squat, another woman, and, a little away, a bald-headed boy whose face was split from ear to ear by an empty grin.

The house had a red tin roof and in the afternoon sun it shone like a sheet of glass.

It was March.

The coolie considered the pile of luggage at his feet, wondering if there was more to follow. Silence spun out, and only the pony fidgeted. The four people in the passage stood still against the railing, so still that it seemed they might be posing in the sun for a photograph.

All the doors on the ground floor of the house were closed. A small gate opened on to a garden in front of the house. A tin letter-box hung on one nail from the gate, like a dead bird suspended upside down; it creaked rustily, rocked by the wind. The sound startled the pony, but it soon regained calm, and looked around amiably, albeit with weary, watery eyes.

A movement on the upstairs veranda of the house caught the coolie's eye. A girl emerged from a room, followed by a pigtailed middle-aged man carrying a small canvas bag. His dress and manner suggested he was a servant of the house. As he lumbered along behind the girl, dragging his foot, the wooden floor shook under his tread.

They were coming down the steps, but the girl halted abruptly on the bottom step, as if she had overlooked something. She turned back, scurried to the upstairs veranda and disappeared from view. The coolie stared. The pony swished its tail. The servant lowered the canvas bag on to the ground, and waited, his muddy, blinking eyes focused on the bare, snow-clad, sunlit peaks.

The girl had gone back to her room where a little boy stood, his large eyes flickering, his head tousled, intently gazing at her.

She wanted to tell the boy that she was leaving, but speech eluded her. The boy turned his back to her. She drew closer to him. It was time to leave, yet she stood there listening to his breathing heave across the shared months of winter. She was flooded by memories of days made chilly by the winds off snowy peaks. She closed her eyes, and, despite the afternoon sun, a darkness gathered behind them.

'Kaya! *Orré* Kaya!' she heard someone call her. They were waiting for her — the coolie, the pony, the four people in the passage below, while the mountains around the house gleamed.

One

Kaya opened her eyes, then shut them again. Time dragged by. Her fingers clenched a corner of her quilt. She lay rigid in bed, possessed by a sinister thought that her head had moved round to her feet, towards the door. This, of course, was preposterous: head and feet couldn't possibly be together in one place. She laughed to herself.

'Shh! What's it?'

'Nothing.'

'Then why are you laughing?'

Chhote, her brother, was too young to understand, but he nevertheless nodded his head gravely, always ready to be part of anything mysterious. If he found something too painful to bear, he would transform it into a tantalizing mystery. He could then cope, even play, with it.

He stretched out under the covers.

On the dark veranda outside, the floorboards groaned. The planks resented even the slightest pressure on them. The house was built of sawn logs, and when a wind sprang it shook the whole structure in its frame. The veranda flooring groaned more than it shook, however.

'Who's it?' asked Chhote.

'No one', said Kaya. Still, hope rose in her. Ever since Lama had left, they let themselves imagine things. They would shut the door to Lama's empty room at night, but come away without bolting it. Then they would lie in their beds with bated breath, waiting for the door to be thrown open by the wind, waiting for Lama to emerge and pace up and down the veranda, as she used to when here. They thought they saw her in the moonlight, which poured down the hillside to scatter in a silver dust on their rooftop, the eaves, the veranda. Whenever the veranda flooring shook, their hearts shook with it.

Was someone there?

She sat bolt upright in the dark. In this large house, some door or the other always rattled, and then the roof would shudder. In all this one could weave one's hopes, peer into the past, retrieve it, relive it. Between now and then stretched a world in which everything was possible, so their hope reached out as far as their terror: they swung between the two, from one extreme to the other.

'Someone turned on the light. Did you see it?'

'Which light?'

'The one on the staircase, between the corner room and the gallery.'

'You're crazy', Kaya said, shivering. 'Mangtu switched on the light in a room. A bathroom tap was turned on too. Didn't you hear the sound of splashing water?'

'Splashing water?' Chhote started laughing, but his laughter sounded eerie and frightened. 'What tales you tell, Kaya! It's too much.'

'I heard water running', she insisted, her hackles up. 'I only closed my eyes, not stopped my ears. I heard everything. I heard that too. . . .' There was a tremor in her voice, as if the leap from one concocted story to another created a truth beyond self-deception.

'You're the one who's crazy! But tell me, what else did you hear?' In such moments Chhote was ever-willing to shed his doubts, determined to be Kaya's accomplice in the luminous light of her wonderland.

'I'm crazy? So!' said Kaya, distancing herself from him. 'You think I'm lying?'

'I didn't mean that!' Chhote's voice caught in his throat, plaintive, tearful. 'But you think too much, even about things which aren't there.'

'What's not there? If there's nothing, why are you sitting up in bed? Tell me, what are you doing here? Tell me, Chhote!'

Chhote was tongue-tied. Kaya had never questioned him so sharply before. The two of them had waited for Lama every night in their room when the lights were switched off and the windows opened. The wind whistled outside. Dry October leaves and fallen twigs scraped the roof. Silence, sibilant with echoes off the hills, filled the space between their listening and waiting, and, like hounds, they set out in pursuit of the smells, the voices, the memories buried out of sight like half-chewed bones in the dense woods of their childhood; they returned to chew at the bones again, unseen, in peace, in the dead of night.

Among these bones was one called Lama, their cousin, the daughter of their father's sister. She'd stayed with them for a few months some time ago. She used the room at the other end of the veranda. She was no longer here but her room had not been rearranged, and it seemed she was still present. So much of her remained in the house that it was difficult to accept she wasn't there any more.

Kaya threw back her quilt and tiptoed into the veranda. There was no one there. The dim light over the staircase was on. The stairs led to Mrs Joshua's rooms on the ground floor. In the passage at the top of the staircase several pairs of shoes were arranged in a row — Babu's, Chhote's, her own. In the dim light these seemed to fuse into a strange, shapeless animal with Babu's shoes as its head and her own chappals as its feet. It was usual for everyone in the family to leave their shoes on the landing at night so that Hariya could clean and polish them early the next morning.

She stared at the empty spot at the end of the row of shoes where Lama's chappals used to be. But it wasn't really empty; it had been taken over by a layer of dust. It was odd, she thought, how the void left by people came to be strung together and filled by a strange, tenacious web. Unnoticed, it would wind around Kaya: she was convinced that Lama was still here, somewhere close by, seeing everything although no one could see her.

No, there isn't a void or an empty space, Kaya thought; no one ever goes away.

*

Chhote waited impatiently for Kaya to come back. Finally, he went out too. Everyone else in the house was asleep, but Lama's door swung open and slammed shut in the wind-swept silence. 'Did you see anyone?' he asked Kaya in a whisper: Kaya did not answer. They stood in the dark, their breathing audible. Kaya, alert and watchful, gazed into all the dark corners of the veranda. A trellis girdled the house. Beyond it were the wooded hills that merged into a distant range of high mountains. They could not see the chain of peaks; what they saw were isolated lights. It was difficult to distinguish a streetlight from a star, and when Lama was here the three of them would sit by the bedroom window attempting to do so. Lama once said that if one closed an eye and saw a light twinkle, it was a star; otherwise, it could be a streetlight or a light in a house, or even the eye of an animal.

Lama never saw ghosts or spirits, only animals. All of us are an animal of one kind or another, although we do not see the animal in us, she would say; but sooner or later the time comes when we're face to face with the animal double, and then, whatever we eat, drink or do is not for ourselves but for it, even though we might not admit it out of shame. Lama had no shame, no fear.

Chhote shivered. How long were they going to remain standing out here?

'Shouldn't we go to bed, Kaya?' he said. He preferred not to go back alone. He always suspected that Kaya didn't tell him what she saw when alone. So he'd made it a habit to stick to his sister like a leech. He took no chances: who knew what might happen in his absence? Even if asleep, he'd quickly rouse himself and jump out of bed to trail his sister if he sensed something was about to happen.

But nothing was going to happen, for nothing ever did, Kaya thought. She sighed despairingly, laden with the weariness of the day gone by. She turned towards Chhote and gripped his shoulders, as if demanding to know why he was still there. Didn't he see there was nobody here? Was he so stupid as to believe Lama would somehow appear? She shook him, as if waking him from sleep. Bleary-eyed, Chhote stared at her. He was not angry with Kaya, he only pitied her. Could anything be sadder than being up in the dark so late in the night, sleepless but not beyond sleep, listening to the rattle of doors? Nurturing illusions, probing them for happiness, and ending with something which is neither one nor the other but a dead rat — was there anything in that to be proud of? He wanted to confront her squarely and tell Kaya enough was enough, from now on he'd sleep in Mother's room, she could do as she pleased, he didn't care.

Didn't care? The rat he took for dead opened its eyes and leered, as though claiming it had nine lives and would outlive them both. Chhote's curious, lonely wanderings between hope and despair would then begin anew. He shuffled along behind Kaya, back into their room.

In their room they had two beds, one on either side of a tripod, and a writing desk piled with school books covered in dust. On the tripod lay an assortment of dead butterflies, Cadbury chocolate wrappers, roots. The roots gave off a sweet, herbal scent. Chhote had not acquired this collection by deliberate choice or design; it just happened to be there, an unwilled yet unquestioned part of his life, an inward extension of the outside. The inner and the outer worlds coalesced seemlessly. The outer world was a ceaseless flux, a stream which overran banks without barriers that entered one's being, carrying on its shimmering surface russet plane leaves, bamboo twigs, pine cones. Chhote's collection reflected the varying moods of the seasons. When Ginny was alive, she too contributed her mite. Grasped between her firm canine jaws, she brought animal bones, torn-down nests or clumps of hair to put by in her accustomed place under the desk they called Ginny's corner. The nests, once slimy with broken eggs, now dried and caked, lay in the corner. But Ginny was dead.

It was dark in the room. Neither Kaya nor Chhote dared switch on the light for fear that Mother would wonder what was going on. She might say nothing, though; but that was another matter.

They lay on their beds, without hope, waiting for sleep to overtake them. A wind traipsing down the mountains tapped on their door hesitantly. An old memory swelled into a sob in Kaya's throat. She recalled how Babuji, home from Delhi, knocked on the door before entering; she saw how he stooped over Chhote's bed and stroked his forehead lightly so as not to awaken him; she watched him in the darkness, holding her breath, trying hard not to give herself away even as a fear gnawed at her heart that he might walk out after all, without noticing her. At such moments she felt as if she was on fire, and would sit up to call out to him in agitation: 'I'm over here'. Her father would turn round at once. 'I know, I know,' he would say soothingly; 'I didn't realize you were awake.' She was, of course, wide awake. Every pore in her body was aware of Father in the dark, pleading wordlessly with him to stay, to live with them in the house where they could all see him all the time, always.

'He used to knock in the same way, didn't he? Do you remember, Chhote?'

Chhote remembered. All that was needed was to wind the key and his memories chugged out like a toy train on its tracks, carrying him past wayside stations which more or less resembled one another, year after year, from one season to the next. When Kaya talked about Babuji, the train pulled in at the Summer Station, sun-flooded, nestling among pines, the needle-leaves honed to dazzling sharp points. Summer, Chhote was told, was the season for migration to hill stations, and since Babuji also came home only during summers, Chhote imagined him toiling across ridge after ridge on the way, and he'd be proud of Babuji. It was a pity, though, that the Summer Station was gone in a twinkling during the descent to the plains. Chhote saw what looked like swarms of ants marching downhill in single file among yellowing pines, away towards distant Delhi, Kanpur, Calcutta—faceless cities, but from behind which peered one face: his Babuji's. Yes, Kaya, I remember, he said to himself in the dark; when summer came, he'd knock on the door in just the same way.

'Do you know, Chhote,' whispered Kaya, sharing a secret, her very own, a veritable treasure she'd been hugging to herself unknown to anyone, 'he'll be home during the Christmas holiday.'

Chhote almost started out of his bed. 'How do you know?' he demanded, his eyes lit up. It had never happened before; the train stopped only at the Summer Station, summer after short-lived summer, across a snow-misted interregnum, empty rooms, crooked branches of leafless trees, a seemingly endless expanse without a trace of Babuji anywhere.

Kaya did not think it necessary to answer. Already she had told him too much. She was deterred by a deep-seated superstition that if she aired her secret hope it would not come to pass quite the way she had expected. She was alarmed by the intensity of Chhote's reaction, and retreated hurriedly to bury her treasure underground and flatten the soil above it. Utterly flat, no tell-tale mound, no path uphill or away down the slopes, no snow-bound winter, no summer, only a stark tract where the wind wandered day and night. No one could ever detect the spot where she had buried the last day of their father's last visit.

Babuji's luggage had been loaded on a rickshaw which would take him to the railway station. Kaya stood with Miss Joshua on the veranda downstairs. It was a hot day. The sun filtered through branches in Mrs Joshua's compound and streamed into the veranda. As the coolies salaamed and Mangtu the faithful servant pushed them out of the way in soldierly style, and as the rickshaw-puller in a bright turban rose to his feet in readiness, a miracle happened, which embossed itself instantly on the stones around in a hieroglyph of pain no one else could have deciphered, which was carried about forever afterwards like a cross. That pain, that hope, derived from the unexpectedness of the moment.

At the very last moment, just as the rickshaw was about to pull out, Babu had got down and strode back to the house as if suddenly reminded of something he'd overlooked in his haste. He walked up to Mrs Joshua on the veranda and said his good-byes. 'I was in a hurry,' he laughed apologetically, 'mind you take care of yourself.' Miss Joshua blinked up at him; she was hard of hearing and couldn't even lip-read very well. She thought he was worrying about Kaya. 'Don't worry, she'll be all right,' she reassured him loudly in her thin voice, 'she'll be all right.' But Babu had meanwhile turned towards Kaya — and then the miracle happened. It tore like a flash of lightning across a sky suffused with pain. 'I forgot to tell you, Kaya,' Babu was saying, 'I'll be home during the Christmas holiday.' He then spoke about her mother, about Chhote, but she registered nothing. Breathless, she hung on to just one sentence of his, and before she could recover he was gone. His rickshaw was nearing the hilltop, a black speck of a housefly crawling up and away in the distance.

Kaya had in her grasp a four-anna coin Babu gave her when leaving; it was to be shared with Chhote as usual. But what Babu had confided to her was for her alone; she didn't have to share it with anyone.

'Come in,' Mrs Joshua pulled her in by her hand, 'I've baked a cake for you.'

Mrs Joshua was a skinny, old woman, as stiff as a ramrod. She always wore a woollen hat, from beneath which white hair fell out over her forehead. She lived on the ground floor. It was said that she and her husband took up residence in this mountain town during the First World War. She came to like the town so much that she stayed on after the War, although her husband preferred to go back to England. At first, he visited her once every year or so, but then he called it quits. However, Mrs Joshua still got in her mail from England several newspapers and brochures, and occasionally letters too, which filled her tin letter-box to the brim. But she seldom bothered to collect her mail. The neighbours said, uncharitably, that it was left to Hariya the sweeper, who came in to clean the commode, to clean up her letter-box as well, and they laughed noisily. But Kaya could never share their amusement on this matter.

Mrs Joshua laughed, too, but sarcastically. She ridiculed all those who spent half the year in the mountains and the other half in offices in Delhi. Gypsy clerks, nomads, she dubbed them disdainfully. When the migratory population packed up to leave for the plains, Mrs Joshua sat on her veranda, a walking-stick across her lap, watching with disapproval the bustling coolies, mules, rickshaws — every unpleasant detail. Everyone who left

was, in her eyes, her foe. She waved her walking-stick indig-
nantly. 'Ungrateful lot', she mumbled to herself. When the same
people reappeared in the street the next summer they were
greeted by her self-satisfied smirk: 'Ah, the fools are back again!'
Sullenly, the newcomers plodded past behind the coolies, trying
not to meet her triumphant gaze.

But Mrs Joshua made an exception in Babu's case. She re-
spected him, for he at least left his family behind. It was extraor-
dinary, she thought, that in the whole neighbourhood there was
but one Indian who went away alone. Perhaps that is why she
had a soft corner for the children; when Babu was gone she'd
feel all the more responsible for them. She kept an eye on both
Kaya and Chhote as they wandered about. She took in their
bruised kneecaps, the dust in their hair, the wild-animal look in
their eyes. 'Tch! Tch!' she grimaced, pointing her walking-stick
at them. 'Your father's gone, that's it', she concluded, as if blam-
ing his absence for their wildness. She looked the children over
thoughtfully and made up her mind quickly. 'Come in,' she
invited them ceremoniously, 'I've some cakes for you in the
oven.' Kaya and Chhote quietly followed her in.

'Are you asleep, Kaya?'

'What's it?'

'I'm cold.'

'Here, come over.' Kaya turned over on her side. The wind
had abated. The clothes hanging to dry no longer fluttered. The
tin roof of Mangtu's quarters rang out as horse-chestnuts fell on
it and rolled down its slope. They counted the resonant thuds,
and, sure enough, found an equal number of chestnuts in the
gutter the next morning. These were the last chestnuts of the
season. Before long, the tree would be bare and the roof cluttered
with discoloured yellow leaves. The roof and the leaves on the
roof played their own variations on the noises of the night . . .
until November, when at last they were choked by snow.

'You won't kick me, will you?'

Chhote didn't wait for an answer and jumped out of his bed

happily. The prospect of a warm bed was sufficiently tempting for him to ignore his fear of being kicked. Kaya moved over to make room for him. Chhote crawled in beside her. The bed, it seemed, was apportioned into an icy North Pole and an African continent of warmth. Chhote edged compulsively closer to the domain of warmth but shrank back in humiliation as Kaya pushed him away: 'Can't you keep to your side of the bed?' she snorted. He'd half a mind to clear out but instead dug in his heels, so to speak; besides, it was already beginning to warm up. Soon he was as warm as he had been in Mrs Joshua's sitting room, where thick curtains kept out not only the sun but the cold wind.

In his dreams, Chhote saw Mrs Joshua's room as a stage on which events unfolded one after another, as in a real play. Next morning, when he actually went there, he expected a repeat performance and took a ringside seat, with the air of one who had bought a ticket for a show.

The two children sank into their chairs while Mrs Joshua re-treated behind the curtain over the door to her bedroom. They listened to her pacing up and down, up and down, interminably. Apparently she had forgotten all about them. But the children didn't mind waiting; the quiet of a mellow wintry afternoon, emphasized by Mrs Joshua's monotonous footsteps, had a lulling effect; it unloosened their muscles, weary after the rough-and-tumble of play. Mrs Joshua was a frail old woman, but as she trod to and fro tremors rippled along the floorboards.

At last Mrs Joshua looked in, the curtain gathered to one side in her hand. 'You're still here?' she exclaimed. Her amazement launched Chhote on his fantasizing; to his mind, there was some-thing dreamlike about guests being taunted. He stared at her, fascinated. Kaya held her gaze, daring her, weighing Mrs Joshua's amazement with her own: 'May we leave, Mrs Joshua?'

'No, no! Not yet. Let me bring you some cake and biscuits. How forgetful of me!' Mrs Joshua threw up her hands in self-reproach. As she hurried away to the kitchen Chhote puzzled over the fact that she looked so old and was yet so youthful in her mannerisms and gestures.

'What are you staring at — eat it up!' Mrs Joshua commanded, waving her stick over the plate of pastries and biscuits until the children picked up one or the other thing to eat.

Chhote reached out his hand shyly: if only he could slip off into a corner and nibble his biscuit in peace! The sight of Mrs Joshua's threatening stick killed his appetite. A saving grace though was that Mrs Joshua had her attention focused on Kaya, leaving him to his own resources. He let his eye rove. There was Mrs Joshua's bedroom behind the curtain. Beyond it, to one side, was the kitchen opposite the bathroom where he'd never been. His fancy sniffed about mysterious nooks there. Sometimes he wondered if Mrs Joshua too sat on a commode like lesser mortals. Did white memsahibs also have to do such distasteful things? Impossible, he told himself. Although it was an important question, he dare not discuss it with Kaya. When his gaze returned from dark interiors it latched on to the gramo-phone covered in blue, with what looked like books or ledgers stacked alongside. Once he'd bided his time to make a beeline for the 'ledgers'; on prying one out he found himself face to face with an array of black discs inside that stared back at him through eyeholes in their bellies.

'Mrs Joshua, it's time we went', Kaya said somewhat shame-facedly, for it did not seem right to walk out immediately after disposing of her cake and biscuits.

'You're a very jimmewar girl', Mrs Joshua remarked. She peppered her speech with Hindi words when being funny or sarcastic. 'How is your mother?'

'Very well, thank you, Mrs Joshua.'

'Very well, eh?' Mrs Joshua took off her glasses before looking out of the window at the birch and plane trees. 'She's growing bigger day by day. Haven't you noticed?'

This time Chhote too paid attention. Now that he gave it a thought, his mother had indeed grown bigger over the last few months. But when Mrs Joshua spoke about it they were both ill at ease, as if it were a matter of shame. Their hearts lurched when somebody hauled their household affairs into the open. They feared they would not be able to protect their home from the curious. They didn't mind so long as Mother stayed inside, but when she came out, even if only to the veranda or to Mangtu's quarters, they felt vulnerable — to ridicule, to some nasty or vulgar remark, the kind they heard bandied about in the streets: that *that* could be asked about their mother was beyond their imagination; it was purgatory even to think of it. When Mrs Joshua mentioned Mother's condition, Kaya had a strong urge to drag Chhote out of her room to the kitchen in their own part of the house where she felt safest.

Mrs Joshua tapped on the table with her walking-stick. 'What do you keep brooding about?' She sounded impatient.

'Nothing, Mrs Joshua.' Kaya looked up timidly.

'You were never like this before.'

Kaya felt Mrs Joshua's searching glance on her face. Mrs Joshua had always been here since the earliest days of Kaya's childhood and had watched her grow.

'Well,' Mrs Joshua took a deep breath, 'it's a good thing you got rid of that witch. Don't ever think about her.'

Kaya went on looking at Mrs Joshua in silence. A shadow of a smile, nebulous like a dream, floated up in her large eyes, and her lips parted. Everything in the room, the rustle in the trees beyond the window, the indolent afternoon sun on the hillside — all seemed to converge on a single point of brilliance: The Witch.

'Mrs Joshua,' Kaya asserted, a strange, rueful smile in her eyes, 'she was not a witch, and I know you know it.'

'I know what you know!' Mrs Joshua was livid with anger. 'Tell me, wasn't it Lama who wrote that letter? Did she or did she not?'

'Which letter, Mrs Joshua?' Chhote asked as he ate another biscuit.

'You be quiet', Mrs Joshua said, casting Chhote a scathing glance. 'Let Kaya speak.'

Kaya, still smiling, showed little interest in Mrs Joshua's question. Perhaps she was not even listening. Perhaps she couldn't have from where she had withdrawn into the charmed circle Lama had drawn round her. Nothing ever reached her there.

'Well, let it be', a disappointed Mrs Joshua conceded wearily. She was confronted by a wilful little waif whose father was away in Delhi, the mother confined to bed and the brother a dreamy puppet. Poor thing! One shouldn't be hard on her.

'Has he started going to school?' Mrs Joshua asked, looking in Chhote's direction; he dunked the last slice of cake in Ovaltine before eating it.

Kaya laughed slightly in derisive disapproval. 'Not yet. He will, next summer.'

'Next summer, is it?' Mrs Joshua's face sagged. Wrinkles dug crisscrossing paths under her eyes, along her nose and across her chin. 'Who knows whether I'll still be here then.'

Chhote stayed his hand. The cake in his mouth melted on its own. 'Are you going somewhere, Mrs Joshua?'

Mrs Joshua smiled. 'Have you seen the cemetery near Sanjauli? My brother is there. I'd like to go to him.'

For many years thereafter, Kaya couldn't forget those calm words spoken by Mrs Joshua of a calm afternoon. How did she know? How could one foretell the moment of one's death? Kaya didn't believe her. People went to offices, moved house — but not Mrs Joshua: she would forever be there in her ground-floor semi-dark flat, rooted to her place, as everlasting as the hills Kaya had known since the first stirrings of her memory. These curtains, these trees, this gramophone — would they let someone so united to them ever part?

Chhote had fallen asleep. Kaya walked out noiselessly across the hall and past Mother's bedroom, its musty silence punctuated by her breathing. She groped her way along the wall to the kitchen.

The glass pane in the door was frosted. She wiped a spot with her fingertip and looked in. She saw Mangtu hunched on a low plank stool, his pigtails bouncing as he scraped ash off the cinders picked up with a pair of tongs from the clay hearth: a box-framed glass-fronted picture of a frozen moment.

She knocked gently. Just once. And again. Mangtu froze. He sat still, as if unable to make up his mind whether to ignore the knock or get up to answer it. In the past he had often sent Kaya away with his studied indifference. But tonight he put aside the tongs, got slowly to his feet and unlatched the chain on the door.

Kaya slipped in swift as a cat before Mangtu could change his mind, and flopped down on a gunny sack spread out beside the sideboard crammed with kitchen gear.

Mangtu said nothing. He didn't even glance at her, and walked across the kitchen to his almirah and brought out the white sheepskin coat he wore when it snowed. He threw it over Kaya's shoulders without a word. Kaya wrapped it around herself, enveloped in its pleasant aroma, a blend of cumin, turmeric and cardamom. She wondered if living sheep smelled as good.

Back on his plank stool, Mangtu fished out a live coal and tossed it on his palm until it was cool enough for him to lick the ash off. The damp coal would radiate a fragrance. Kaya watched Mangtu in rapt attention; she was tempted to taste the ash, but knew — and she resented it — that Mangtu would not let her.

Mangtu's heavy, laboured breathing and the clatter and scrape of tongs as the blades bit into coal after glowing coal deepened the silence in the room.

'Is Chhote asleep?'

'Yes, he went to sleep ages ago.'

'And you — couldn't you get to sleep?' Mangtu peeled ash off the burnt-out coals without a pause.

Kaya kept silent. Snug in the sheepskin coat, she was no longer bothered about sleep or the lack of it. What mattered was that the fears and doubts which had pursued her during the day were falling back.

'What was Memsahib saying to you?' Mangtu turned his head towards her.

'She . . .' Kaya trailed off. She looked up at him helplessly before dropping her eyes to stare at the cinders in the hearth.

'What did she say?' He looked Kaya full in the face.

'She spoke about Mother.'

Mangtu knitted his brows. 'What did she say?'

'About her growing big.' Kaya turned to him with a look wavering between shame and wonderment.

Mangtu let out a sigh, as if he was sore in all his muscles.

Winter was the worst period of the year, for the aches flared into an agonizing pain in his legs so that he had to continually shift his weight from one hip to the other. His legs were bandaged from ankle to knee in strips of torn cloth tied like a puttee. Kaya never found out whether he did this to keep out the cold or to quell his pain.

'Mangtu . . .'

'Yes?'

'How long will Mother keep growing?'

Mangtu took a coal from the fire and gazed into it long enough to find an answer to the child's curiosity. 'Can't say,' he said at last, 'such things are upto God.'

'What things?'

'Can't you see?' He stretched and yawned so hard that the ash blew off the coal. Of no use to him any more, he returned it to the hearth.

'Once I saw . . .' Kaya laughed quietly. Sometimes her manner of mature solemnity left Mangtu thoroughly bemused.

'What did you see?'

'Mrs Joshua's letter-box. Haven't you?'

Mangtu nodded his head.

'It's always open, you know.'

'What do you want to say?'

'We looked into it once — Chhote and I.'

'You shouldn't have.' Mangtu's breathing whistled in the silence across the kitchen.

'But there was nothing inside. Not a single letter.'

'Poor Memsahib — who would write to her?' Mangtu spoke pityingly, as though it was unfortunate that the woman should not receive letters any more. But a glance at Kaya convinced him that something else was implied, and he went pale. He was a sallow-looking man but at this moment a sickly pallor of alarm gathered in his face. 'What is it, Kaya?' he insisted.

'I climbed up the grille of the gate while Chhote stood below.' Her gaze riveted to the door, Kaya seemed to be unravelling a dream thrown up by memory. 'I climbed up the grille, threw open the letter-box and looked in. There was nothing there except some straw, bird droppings, and dust — lots of it. When

I was about to shut it I'd a feeling someone was watching me . . . someone from within the letter-box.'

Mangtu threw her a quick glance, and, groaning, got up slowly from his low plank stool. He took a kettle from a drawer of the sideboard and put some water to boil on the hearth.

'You're sure you remember it right?' Mangtu spoke up after a while. Kaya sat huddled against the wall. He could neither believe nor disbelieve her. A simple man from the mountains, he didn't trust his suspicions nor suspect what the other trusted. For him, an occurrence didn't have to come to pass to be there — it just *was*: it was there in a state of suspension between happening and non-happening, neither impossible nor yet real; something inevitable, which no one could will or wish away. He thus never asked Kaya whether what she said had in fact happened, or whether she'd merely made it up. For him, the thought was as good as the actual, the two overlapped: each was as much the truth as the other, fore-ordained, predestined; there was no room for any doubt, even as it was beyond comprehension.

'Is it true, Kaya, that someone was watching you?' Mangtu wanted to make sure all the same.

'Of course, it's true! I saw an eye staring back at me . . . and I slammed the letter-box shut on it at once. But the eye still held on to me.' Kaya's eyes were closed. Like a sleepwalker, she seemed to go right up to the edge of the roof, beyond which there was nothing except wind and darkness.

Wind and darkness. Lord, the wind during those days! Babu was away in Delhi. Mother was swelling under her smock. I wandered about the house. Once I opened Mrs Joshua's letter-box. Chhote stood below steadying the gate for me. 'Can you see anything?' he asked. 'Yes, bird droppings, straw . . . and an eye peering out of it.' A single eye, up in the back, devouring the world at large. You don't believe me, Mangtu — isn't it? You think I'm mad. Go and see it for yourself, it's still there. Go out and open the gate. The letter-box remains open at night. It will be in there — that eye, wide awake and white and growing old in its socket of straw. It's been there all along.

'What's been there, Kaya?' Mangtu's voice reached her as though from a great distance. 'What is it?'

✳

As the kettle on the hearth simmered, Mangtu's shadow was woven into the spiralling steam. It struck Kaya that she had come to the furthest end of the house. The window in front of her, which gave on to Jakhu Hill, was open to let out the smoke from the hearth. Beyond it, stars shone in the muted, diffuse bluish darkness of a cold October night. A breeze rustled in the chestnut tree; it rose only to be intercepted by tree after tree until the forest chanted in unison all around.

Mangtu took off the kettle and emptied it into a hot-water bottle held by Kaya. He then stoppered the bottle before wrapping it up in a napkin, rather as though he were putting a baby to bed. He gave it to Kaya.

'You want me to come with you?'

Kaya stood uncertainly with the bottle held to her chest. Mangtu stepped ahead to open the inner door for her. Kaya walked out alone from the kitchen and into the drawing room, where the wind ballooned up the faded blue cotton matting. It was perhaps the most neglected room in the house, lying in its middle like a patch of uninhabited desert, cold and unpeopled, the fireplace unlit. With Babu's departure, the sofa chairs were covered by sheets and the rug rolled up against the wall. The matting stretched bare across the floor, ruffled by wind — only now it looked more like a lake in which Chhote pretended to swim until either the wind dropped or Mrs Joshua downstairs stamped out into the yard on her walking-stick. 'Stop it, for heaven's sake, will you? You'll cause an earthquake!' she screamed, waving her stick threateningly while her white hair streamed out from under her hat — a prophet of the desert: 'What's going on over there?' Whereupon Chhote, cowering behind the trellis and looking warily down at her, answered: 'We were swimming, Mrs Joshua.' Chhote was a stickler for truth: 'We were swimming across the matting.' Wide-eyed, Mrs Joshua glared at him: 'Swimming, did you say? Have you converted the room into a swimming pool?' A tearful Chhote did his best to explain: 'No, no, Mrs Joshua! It's the billowy matting we were swimming on.' He watched helplessly as Mrs Joshua seemed to crumple to the ground, groaning, her head between her hands. He couldn't quite grasp what relation his matting or make-believe pool bore to Mrs Joshua's intense suffering.

Mangtu was annoyed when, having cleaned up the kitchen for the night, he came upon Kaya dawdling in the middle of the sitting room, the hot-water bottle held absent-mindedly to her chest. 'What are you doing here? Don't you realize she must be waiting?' he said angrily.

Kaya started. This was not the first time she had been caught. More often than not, she paused in the sitting room on her way to Mother. In that moment the memories of past summers came crowding upon her, even as ghosts stepped out from dark corners to lure her, to whisper in her ears insistently what she'd heard before, time and again.

She shook off the ghosts, walked past them, and turned right to the door under which a rib of light gleamed. She knocked on the door before bursting into the room.

Her eyes dropped to the bed in which her mother lay, a bedside lamp picking out her pillow and head, and the shadow on the wall which appeared more real than the person herself.

'So it's you!' The head on the pillow turned upwards to face her. 'You're late tonight.'

No hint of anger, petulance or protest. Only a certain weariness which never diminished nor grew: it always remained the size of the bed — indeed, the bed seemed to personify it. Kaya bent forward as two hands rose from the bed to accept the hot-water bottle. 'Please put it under my feet — they're very cold', her mother said with a wan smile. Kaya placed the bottle under her feet, struck anew by their smallness. They were smaller than her own feet, and lay shivering one upon the other, the red rubber bottle a small consolation, a mere sop to the cold, yet an island of warmth and happiness before long. Kaya was possessed by a mad longing to snuggle up between her mother's feet within the nest of the quilt. But her hands drew back, slipping off the bottle in the bed. She shivered in the cold. Her mother's voice reached her like a stranger's from the other side of darkness; it rapped gently on the wall between them: 'Is Chhote asleep?' Then she saw her mother peering closely at her.

'Yes, he is. I was in the kitchen.'

'Wouldn't he be frightened if he woke to find himself alone?' her mother observed hesitantly, ashamed of her fear. She feared dogs, Tibetan mendicants, Chinese pedlars. She turned pale with fear if anyone entered her room without knocking.

'No, he won't get up — he sleeps like a log.' Kaya felt restive when comforting her mother, as if she were deceiving her. Her mother tended to believe such tales as she might tell, so even an innocuous little lie left an unpleasant taste in Kaya's mouth.

'Any letters in the post?'

'None. Were you expecting any?'

'Not really.' Her mother hesitated. 'Your Bua hasn't written for a long time.'

'Is she supposed to visit us?' Kaya's heart throbbed in expectation.

'Why,' her mother looked up eagerly, 'have you heard anything of the sort?' She was more than willing to place her trust in her daughter.

Kaya let her head drop. The shadow on the wall moved. The mother shrank into herself.

'Listen.'

Her mother turned to look up. 'What is it, Kaya?'

'If Bua comes, will Lama be with her?'

The mother nodded. She reached out her hand to Kaya, shivered at the contact and withdrew. 'You're so cold, Kaya!'

Kaya sat lost at the edge of the bed. She registered neither her mother's touch nor what see had just said. Lama must be in Meerut, Kaya thought; how long and steep is the descent beyond Kalkaji to the plains? There must be a vast level tract below, rather like the Annandale ground up here, strung out with cities right up to the ocean. . . . Kaya hoped she'd look down one day from the Hanuman temple on top of Jakhu Hill, the highest peak hereabouts, to see if she could, on a clear cloudless day, see Meerut, even spot the house in which Lama lived. She wondered whether Lama would hear her if she shouted to her to come. It might be possible, she told herself. Mangtu said voices carried far in the hills; where he came from, people in far-flung hamlets simply called out to one another if they had to: there was silence there, all over and so deep that no call went unanswered.

There was silence here, too, in this room. But Mother called out to no one. Or even if she did, nobody heard: everyone carried on blissfully convinced that she never called out to anyone.

'Isn't it time you went to bed?' her mother said slowly. 'It's late already.'

No, no, not already — not yet, Kaya said to herself; there was no hurry, for the nights in winter are long. The lamplight fell on Mother's averted face. She looked very pale. Locks of her straggly hair had caught under her pillow. She opened her eyes every once in a while to see if Kaya was still there. She had insisted on her leaving, but was reassured all the same by her presence, for Kaya had the power to protect her from her fear of impending disaster.

A selfish thought, and the mother was ashamed of it — but she was anxious her daughter should not feel bored, so she forced a smile and said: 'Kaya, did I tell you that Lama was married? She's very happy now and takes full care of her household.'

Kaya, who was watching her mother's lips move, didn't trust her ears when the word 'happy' issued forth; she thought it was a lie, a falsification. Then it occurred to her that it was probably the truth as Mother saw it: to her, the four walls of a house symbolized happiness, for beyond them the world was oppressive, callous, stone-hearted. Mother had always been worried about, and terrified of, Lama who, she said, couldn't be trusted: she might get herself into trouble: better if she had her own hearth to tend. Mother would frighten Bua with her own fears about Lama: 'Look, marry her to the first boy you can find or you'll live to rue the day.' Bua was also worried: 'Where are the boys? How can I find one?' Hearing this, Kaya was astonished: how was it Bua could find no boy when the streets overflowed with them, playing about, going to school . . . they were everywhere!

Kaya pulled away from her mother. A fury raised its hood within her. If only Mother hadn't importuned Bua, Lama would still have been here, in her room, now haunted by the wind, empty. One day she opened the door and had found Lama gone.

But Lama is still over there, by the railway track, where the midday sun struggles to disentangle itself from the bushes and the green poison ivy, between hills on either side crouched in the dry colourless air. I look about for Lama, taking my clues from rustling bushes. Sometimes I see her legs naked below the hem of her salwar, hitched up above her knees. She wears her dupatta round her waist like a sash. Her stringy unbound hair falls all over her shoulders. She emerges from the bushes to walk up the gleaming railway line. We veer up the hillside to a yellowing grass patch which opens out like a raised palm close to the hump over the dank darkness of the tunnel through which the track runs. It's difficult to climb to the hump. Lama gets there ahead of me. She pulls me up by my arm and gathers me in her lap, but I jump off at once and look into her big eyes staring through the grass at me. All round rise the hills, and the railway track runs below. We lie on the grass, our ears to the ground, waiting for the train, but what we hear is the rumble of the wind in the tunnel. . . . One day as we lay there, she clutched my hand, screaming something at me, but I couldn't hear her in the roaring clatter of train wheels. When the train was gone and silence returned to the hills, I turned to Lama. 'What was it you were trying to tell me?' 'Nothing', she said, laughing. 'You heard something?'

It seemed to Kaya that she was still swinging on Lama's laughter, out in the cold, beyond the warmth of her mother's body and the hot-water bottle, above the dark tunnel heaving with her mother's breathing, an arm thrown across her face — and then she heard Mangtu's voice reach her from far-off, sending her tumbling down the hump, away, further away from Lama's screams.

'Wake up, Kaya', Mangtu shook her gently. 'Go and sleep in your own bed.' She got up, surprised that she had fallen asleep on her mother's pillow. She stumbled dazedly down uneven slopes of sleep to level ground and let herself be led across the sitting room and the passage beyond to her bed which stood empty and cold in the pale moonlight. Chhote turned over, blinked dreamily, wondered where he was and if Kaya was there in her bed alongside his — but this surfacing from deep slumber on a wintry night was very nearly a dream in itself, a continuum, just a pit or a log, an obstacle that sleep jumped clear of in a trice to claim him again. But Kaya's sleep had vanished. Her loneliness, anger, yearning and despair interwove to form a globular mass of mist which was neither so soft that it would dissolve in tears nor so malleable as to be moulded into the solace of wise counsel. The mist rose into the bar of moonlight that fell across her bed, and as Mangtu turned away after tucking her in she caught hold of the edge of his coat, pleading: 'No, don't leave yet! Please!' Mangtu looked around hesitantly over the grubby moonlight between the two beds, his old bones rattling under Kaya's tugging, trembling hands. 'What a girl', he growled. 'There's nothing to be afraid of. Nothing at all.' It seemed it was not Mangtu but someone else, his soul beneath his rags perhaps, which was groaning, and wheedling Kaya: 'There, there's nothing to be afraid of. Nothing to be afraid of at all!' He intoned the words like a charm, a sort of litany, over and over again, as if it was not Kaya but himself he was reassuring. Lulled by Mangtu's somnolent mumblings, Kaya's grip on his coat relaxed, her arm swung over the side of the bed, her fist unclenched, and one more friable day ran out through her fingers like gritty sand.

Two

They were slowly climbing up the steep road. Bua stopped at each windy wooden havaghar by the wayside to recoup. She slumped on the bench, took out her paan box, crushed tobacco in her palm, tossed the powder into her mouth, tucked in her white cotton sari at the waist — and was ready again for the next leg of the seemingly unending walk uphill.

They were on their way to Falkland, Kaya's uncle's house.

Kaya hung on to Bua's finger. If she bounded ahead or fell behind, Bua, out of breath, screamed at her, 'Don't you run up and down, Kaya! Here, stay by my side, will you?' Kaya watched Bua's fish mouth gasping for air in wonder. The wind had disarranged Bua's cotton sari; the billowy hem lashed about her bared, dark spindly shins. Kaya burned with shame. 'Pull your sari down over your legs, Bua!' she cried. 'Why such embarrassment, little one?' Bua retorted, 'What's so shameful, eh? Is anybody watching us?' An outraged Kaya dragged Bua up the slope that deserted afternoon, the pines on the hillside fluttering in the wind, and she herself anxious lest some passer-by take Bua for her mother. Near the top of the slope she let go of Bua and walked ahead, as if she had nothing to do with her. In another moment she turned round and saw Bua stagger along forlornly. She stamped back to her, exasperated. 'Can't you see I'm tired? I'm dog-tired', she fumed, angry with herself for worrying about Bua. 'I can't go on and on; I need a rest — do you hear?' Kaya reckoned that if only Bua sat down, her sari would naturally fall in place again over the shame of her shrivelled legs.

They sank down side by side on a bench in the shelter at the end of the incline. Bua faced the road, Kaya the hillside sprinkled with clusters of trees, bushes, houses. The girl's gaze lingered on the rooftops of the Lower Bazar below, the church on the Ridge, the Jakhu peak that rose above the town. The landscape, chequered by sunshine and shade, looked like a huge chessboard complete with white and black figures set opposite each other.

'It looks like a dead town', said Bua.

'In what way?'

'Just look at the ravenous months of those demonic rocks all around. . . . I can't understand how your mother lives here the whole year round.'

All year round, through the blur of the summer sun, the falling leaves, the prolonged rains — the long nights when hailstones pelted the roof before snow fell white against the darkness, the flakes piling silently outside the window where I sat staring out with Chhote . . . all year round: I wondered if everything the window showed could ever be pigeonholed in this or that month of the year.

No, not really. What she saw through her window seemed to have no end, no tag — and so it could neither be catalogued nor parcelled out according to seasons. That only plainsmen did; they brought with them their own sense of the passage of time. Bua, too, came from the plains — from a place called Meerut. She owned a house there, left to her by her dead husband. She lived in it with Lama. She came to the mountains rather reluctantly twice a year, to visit both her brothers for a month each. It baffled her how, of all the places across the length and breadth of India, the two brothers should have struck upon this place, away from all their relations, where nothing seemed to move but the trees on the hills and the monkeys in the trees. Even more frustrating than their choice of this desolate town was that they lived in far-flung houses — one near the top, the other almost at the base of the hill. Trudging the deserted roads between their homes seemed to unhinge all the joints in her body. She'd had a difficult time bringing up Lama all by herself; after her husband's death life had suddenly loomed ahead like a sheer cliff, but that had been easier to negotiate — mere child's play — than this stretch of road. Had there been no halting spots along the way, or Kaya's companionship, she'd have fallen apart in negotiating it.

'Why don't you hire a rickshaw?' Chachaji would say. Bua always tended to make light of the suggestion. No one but Kaya knew of the exhibition she put on at the rickshaw stand. All the rickshaw-pullers, almost to a man, could now recognize her from a distance. When the rickshaw-pullers saw her inch along the road holding Kaya's hand, they would swiftly go past her, tinkling their bells as they went, looking round to watch the effect. This was so unlike the earlier days when they crowded round her as she strutted like Napoleon from one to another with Kaya in tow, raising her offer of fare anna by embarrassing anna, as if bidding at an auction. The bidding crawled along as she went back and forth at a snail's pace, until it reached eight annas. The hike from that point to the two rupees demanded by the rickshaw-pullers raised insuperable problems, and Kaya would then burst into tears. 'Come on, Bua, we'll walk', she would plead, tugging at her. But Bua ignored her, still shuffling from one rickshaw-puller to another to yet another, her gaunt legs visible below her billowing sari, the loose-end pallu slipping off her bosom time and again: she certainly made a spectacle of herself. At last one or other rickshaw-puller would lose his temper and quip, 'Take my advice, lady — hire a pony. It'll be cheaper and faster. Besides, you'll look like Rani Durgavati astride it.' Within no time, then, the rickshaws scattered and Bua stared emptily at the emptied stand. Turning to Kaya she said: 'They've no patience, those men. How soon they give up. I'd have been willing to pay one more anna.'

But there was no one available to hear Bua for the moment. Even Kaya had moved away. Bua cast about her, grumbling to herself. The hills seemed to close in. Fear constricted her throat. 'Kaya! Orré Kaya!' she shouted after her. Her cry echoed back to her from the hills like a wandering spirit. Kaya rushed back. 'We're already halfway there, Bua. Look, we can see the Kali temple!'

✳

Bua lay down in the courtyard of the temple, her head pillowed on a small bundle she was carrying. Kaya turned the tap at the entrance of the shrine and let the icy water wash away the fatigue of the long climb.

'Tired — are you, Kaya?'

Kaya nodded vaguely, trapped between truth and falsehood. A 'no' would have been a lie, and she was wary of saying 'yes', for if Bua knew how worn out she was she'd refuse to take her along to Chachaji's the next time — and that would be awful. She therefore struck a balance, a compromise, between the two: 'I'm tired, yes — but not all over.'

'What do you mean?'

'Only my legs are tired.'

'Only the legs, eh?' And Bua who never laughed, who always looked tense and anxious, broke into a peal of laughter that reminded Kaya of another time as it bounced off the temple walls. Kaya stared into her face suspiciously: Bua's laugh was exactly like Lama's.

'Why are you looking at me like that? What's the matter?'

'Nothing.' Kaya turned away. 'We'd come to this temple when Lama was here.'

'Oh!' Bua lay back again. She steadied her eyes. The brass bell over the entrance swung in the breeze.

'What did you do here?' Bua asked slowly.

'We'd play. Didn't Lama tell you?'

Lama, Kaya and Chhote used to come to the temple on winter evenings. There were few devotees here then; most would leave after the arati. Only the pujari stayed back in his accustomed place near the idol of Kali. A covered walkway ran around the hall and the three of them played hide-and-seek in its dark corners, running ecstatically around the shrine.

Kaya recalled vividly one such evening. They were playing after the evening arati was over and it was Lama's turn to hide. Both Kaya and Chhote looked for her everywhere but couldn't find her. Chhote finally gave up and slumped down beside the pujari. Kaya too was on the point of giving up when she caught sight of a huddled shape deep in a niche, and stopped in her tracks.

'Is that you, Lama?' she called out.

'Come here.' Lama held her gaze.

She went over to her.

'Will you do me a favour, Kaya?'

'What's it?' She was more than willing to do anything for Lama.

Lama held out an envelope. 'Will you please pass this on to your mother after I'm gone?'

'Is it a letter?'

'Just give it to her, and don't say it's I who gave it to you.'

'What should I tell her if she asks?'

'Tell her some unknown man pressed it into your hand.'

As Kaya stared in disbelief, Lama wrapped an arm round her.

'Tomorrow we'll go for a trek along the railway line', Lama promised. 'We'll take Ginny with us. Now, what do you say to that?'

Three

It was a close, cloudy day; even the air didn't stir. Cliff-faced peaks loomed over the town cloaked in greyness.

We were going down the hill.

I stopped for a moment, noting the listless, cheerless, grimy sun. The tunnel rose from a clump of grass above us. Ginny ran off, down the railway track below. A nightmare, this keeps returning in unsuspected ways to haunt me. I can hardly believe that I am the same Kaya.

From where I stood I could see the long shed of the station. Electric poles ran apace with the trees for some distance before disappearing into the forest beyond. Nearer at hand, the track coiled out from the tunnel to loll in a patch of sunshine.

I was in the middle, with Ginny far ahead, and Lama far behind. Lama was whistling: the sound sped through the air, sometimes seeming quite near, sometimes far-off. As I turned to look for Lama, I almost ran into her. She wore her dupatta round her neck, knotted below the throat; the parting in her hair was grey with dust. The dust specked her eyebrows too, but her fluttering eyelids had managed to keep it at bay. Her wide, dilated eyes, hard and watchful, gave nothing away.

Without a word to each other, we continued on our way down. We drew up at a familiar boulder much as draught horses do at their wonted destination. We had often lazed the afternoon away on that rock. The Simla-Kalka shuttle clattered by, spewing smoke which billowed towards us or floated away down into the valley. In the distance the smoke-cloud looked like another boulder — a huge one. The one we sat on wasn't very large;

we could easily climb on to it — except Ginny, who went around it in circles helplessly wagging her tail, clawing at the rock agonizingly, until, defeated, she sprawled out flat near by. She had a slim frame, and for hair black and white daubs which fused into a crescent at her throat. She always held her head bent forward, not so much because she was lazy, but because she endlessly sniffed for some buried treasure, some great secret that she must unearth. Her tongue hung out in this ceaseless quest, red as a stained paan leaf, saliva dribbling as drops of sweat. No matter where Ginny wandered off in the bushes, we could track her by the trail of her spittle.

The first time I saw Ginny she lay listless on Mrs Joshua's veranda, perhaps dying, a ball of white, a white crescent at her throat. I took her in for a hot bath and a vigorous scrub but the half moon didn't wash out. Instead, it emerged a clearer white, reaching out to her forehead, a natural caste-mark. Ginny then stayed on with us. She probably once had a master who abandoned her when going off to Delhi at the end of the summer — as most people did, leaving their pets behind on deserted verandas to fend for themselves, or in the cold streets during the bitter nights; but when I washed her clean, her past attachments too seemed to have been washed off.

Sometimes we forced open Ginny's eyes, with Chhote clasping her kicking legs. Lama would part her eyelids one after the other — and a glistening moist blob, with our reflections in it, swam across her pupils. 'Do you know what that light in her eyes is? It's her soul', Lama declared. And I asked myself which one was the soul — that which reflected our images, the jelly-like thing over the pupils, or that which animated her protesting legs. We felt guilty after treating Ginny like this, as though in prying out her soul from her eyes we had done Ginny a grave wrong for which there could never be atonement.

But Ginny wasn't in the least unhappy. She followed Lama everywhere, as if Lama held her soul in her palm. At night she lay shivering outside Lama's room, her claws raking the closed door continually. Even though Lama never allowed her in, sustained by some obscure hope, Ginny did not give up.

Some secret fascination must have lured Ginny every night

past all the open rooms in the house to the closed doors of Lama's room.

But that afternoon Ginny was running down the slope. She probably thought we were heading for our rock as usual. She scampered past the bushes towards the tunnel where the rails gleamed in the sunlight. From afar she looked like a ball of wool rolling down. Then there was nothing. Only the bushes, the trees, and a stealthy shadow of a cloud closing in over two peaks to swallow the valley.

The whistling stopped. The air moved.

'Did you hand over the letter I gave you?' Lama whispered, aiming the question at me without any warning, the way she confronted me in the Kali temple.

I straightened my head. She was sitting on the rock, facing the tunnel.

'No one believed a word in it', I answered.

Lama raised a dusty eyebrow but the gaze that fixed on me was calm.

'They will some day, I tell you!'

Some day. But we were running out of time. Lama would soon be going to Meerut. We kept a count of the days. She had drawn ninety lines on the wall and crossed out one each day. By now the wall was full of crosses, each a summer day spent together. When Lama arrived the plane trees in Mrs Joshua's garden were just beginning to put out new leaves. These had since turned russet, yellow or reddish brown. As the lines on the wall continued to be scored out and the trees shed their coloured leaves, letters arrived from Bua. Everything had finally been settled, she wrote: a boy had been found after much difficulty, and now she wanted to be free of the responsibility of looking after her daughter as soon as she returned home. What was so difficult about this, I asked Mother; there were boys galore. She laughed: 'Silly! You don't find boys in the mountains, do you?' But one saw boys all the time — going to school, buzzing like houseflies in the bazaar. . . . So many, but still none good enough for Lama!

'You wrote that letter, didn't you, Lama?' I sat near her.

'So you told them?'

'I didn't. I told Mother that a man had given it to me. She didn't believe me, though. She took it to Mrs Joshua. Mrs Joshua read it, and said it was all fake.'

'Fake, is that what she said?' Lama's eyes flared with anger. 'What does that wrinkled white woman know?' But she patted my hair gently and for a while only the sound of bushes rustling in the breeze disturbed the silence.

'Do you still have that letter?' Lama eventually asked.

'I keep it in my pocket.' I held out the crumpled envelope. She didn't even glance at it, just nodded, and said, 'Read it'.

'You mean you didn't write it yourself?'

Lama made no answer. Her gaze was riveted on the railway track.

'Shall I read it, then?'

Lama nodded again. I began to read aloud in the deep silence that filled the afternoon. *Someone is deceiving you. Perhaps you don't know but the man you are going to marry this girl to is too old for her. He is blind and deaf. He is a widower. His wife died barely six months ago. Poor woman, how she suffered! Everyone knows about it except the mother of this girl who, blind to reason, is determined to send her daughter to her doom. A man who thinks nothing of marrying again within six months of the death of his wife — how can he ever be expected to make this girl happy? The spirit of his dead wife still lives in the house; it will destroy the young bride. Mind you, there's still time. If you have the good of the girl at heart, don't make her go back to Meerut, for, remember, it will be as good as deliberately pushing her into the jaws of death. There can be no greater sin than this. Desist from sin, and leave the girl alone. Remember Meerut means* DEATH. Below it was a drawing of a grinning skull and an arrow. Opposite the arrowhead was scrawled *Meerut.*

'Is that all?' said Lama seeming surprised that the letter had been finished so soon and there was nothing more in it.

'They won't send you back now.'

'Why?'

'To such a man? How could they?' I looked at her: perhaps she had already worked out a solution; perhaps she would find one before it was too late. But she sat still, looking nowhere, turned to stone, a rock perched on another rock.

At last she turned to me, a thin smile on her lips.

'It's all lies', she said. 'Through and through.'

She snatched the letter from me, and tore it slowly into bits. The fragments floated down towards the railway track.

I looked at the tunnel — one afternoon we had sat near it and Lama shouted out to me even as her words went under the wheels of the train. I couldn't hear what she said. Often, I didn't hear her very well and sometimes it seemed that she, rather than I, belonged here in the mountains, and it was odd that I would continue to live here while she would have to leave one day — far from the Kali temple, this railway track, the forested hill.

'I will not go!' Lama declared one evening on the dark veranda. We'd just got back home. Ginny was already at her door. Below, a pale light from Mrs Joshua's window scattered on the trees in the small garden. 'Look here, Kaya,' she urged, 'don't ever lock up my room: I live in it, and will continue to do so forever.'

'Aren't you going back to Meerut?'

'I must', she conceded. 'But I'll be here too. They won't even know.'

'Will we be able to see you?'

'Why not? You'll find me beside you every night.'

It was very quiet; only the floorboards under our feet creaked. Ginny watched us with her bright eyes. Occasionally she broke into a whining howl, as if she'd seen a shadow move among the trees. But soon she'd become calm again, comforted by Lama's presence.

'Open your fists', Lama coaxed. I let my fingers uncurl and she squeezed my hands. 'Promise me you won't tell anyone', she said under her breath. 'Tell what, Lama?' She must have noticed the amazement in my eyes and been moved by the fear in my expression. She peered at me in the darkness. 'You believe in the existence of the soul, don't you?' I nodded. Those days I'd readily go along with anything as long as I was left alone: it was the easy way out — and safer. 'Well, when you open Ginny's eyes you see something don't you?' she persisted. *It struck me then that playing safe was not enough, there was something else, too, besides ourselves, something both within and beyond us — another self — that cried out to be saved.* 'You know how Ginny suffers? She keeps howling outside my door at night. . . . Don't you ever hear anything?' She laughed quietly, but the laugh seemed to rise not from her throat but from some wind-swept hollow. 'You're a selfish girl!' She wrung my hands. 'Listen, Ginny wants release — as I do: I want to get out. Do you know how to go about it?' A numbness spread through me. The vestiges of the happiness in me were instantly clipped as though by pincers and doused in cold water. Release? That can't be found — it is given.

'It's the train', said Lama. There was a distant rumble behind the hills, faint at first, then louder, as if a huge boulder had started moving unhurriedly towards us — unseen, but its sound echoing all around.

We scrambled off our rock, and walked through tall, yellowing grass towards the tunnel. The pine-needless carpeting the slope had made it rather slippery. Our descent was slow and cautious.

There were no rocks here, only the grass that rose above us, and the bushes, and pines among the bushes. These stood motionless. It was a quiet hour of the afternoon when a drowsy silence descends upon this mountain town. Neither the breeze nor what it passed over made any sound.

'Where's Ginny?' Lama's lips twitched; her voice came out strained and hurried like a little child's before a bout of coughing, which involved remote memories of sweltering days and darkened rooms.

Ginny lay on her belly facing the tunnel, her head bent forward, eyes closed, tongue out to one side of the long pointed fang. She looked quite at peace, sure that we were somewhere near by. As we approached, she held her breath for a moment, then realizing that it was the two of us, she began breathing evenly again.

'Ginny!' Lama called out. 'Ginny!' Her voice had a strange edge to it, but there was nothing in her manner for me to worry about. Ginny stood up on hearing her name, stretched, shook off traces of lethargy, and looked uncertainly about her as she tried to locate the direction of the call. She started climbing down slowly towards the tunnel.

Ginny climbed down, as if in sleep, hugging her shadow on the slope. She stopped short of the tunnel, looked ahead and behind her, sniffing the air for danger . . . it was then that I realized I was alone.

I turned round. Lama was no longer there. The tall grass, bushes, leaves on the ground, the long shadows of trees — everything looked just as it had a moment earlier. But the air quivered as the wires slung between the poles across the hills suddenly came alive, setting off reverberations dark as the smoke over the valley.

Ginny was not far from me. But the distance between us spun out as she went down in a trance towards the sounds pouring from the dark tunnel. She moved as if mesmerized, looking neither to her left nor right, as though she'd at last picked up in the tremulous bushes by the mouth of the tunnel the scent of the cache she'd been looking for all her life. I was too dazzled by the sun in my eyes to see clearly, but I was aware of the bright black and white spots on the body of a receding Ginny, and of the welter of sound from the tunnel: a blend of intimidation, endearments, command and, above all — though I didn't discover this until much later — compassion more than pity or sorrow, that transcended the reality of dying or of death or of being put to death, unconcerned with the dizzying gust in the middle before the dust settled down . . . and everything was over.

To say that I understood all of this then would be untrue: it was beyond my comprehension. I merely saw the lines strung out between the poles away across the two paired hills, over which a flock of birds flew away.

All this I can see again, recall, repeat to myself. There was Ginny crawling down the slope, stopping short of the railway track as though her legs had buckled under her, her snout raised towards the tunnel from which came the frantic call — *Ginny! Ginny! Ginny!* — tugging at her like the end of a rope even while she, bewitched, stared into the deep darkness, her ears twitching, her tail striking helplessly against the rail. . . . Who was there? Who was calling her from the other side?

I stood rooted to my spot, drained, spellbound. That sound

was fated to wind round my legs, truss Ginny up. In a daze I realized that I too was screaming — even as that scream tore through me, I felt detached from myself, listening to it from the outside, although by now all sound had ceased: there was only the sun over the distant knolls. A hush spread from the hills to fill the sky before the train crashed out from the tunnel, a heaving, churning blur, a furious dragon spouting smoke. In another blinding moment, it disappeared behind the other hill, leaving behind nothing, a nothingness, time spinning to a standstill, a living creature running for its life between the rails, a little ball of wool, a splash of a half-moon in the air, fur tufted with blood — all of which is a memory, a nightmare that keeps returning. I return to this day, and wait again by the gaping tunnel: first there's the smoke, then the roar of the wheels, then the impatient panicky call from behind the bushes — *Ginny! Ginny! Ginny!* But that, too, subsides with the dying whimper.

Nothing happened for a very long time. I did not stir from my foothold. The sun had faded. I noticed a movement in the bushes behind the tunnel, and saw the top of Lama's head emerge, then the face. A Lama I'd not seen before rambled along as if lost in a dream, strangely unbothered, like an animal in the wilderness unmindful of its surroundings. She walked up the track, her dupatta girding her waist like a belt, the baseband of her salwar muddied. In her hand she held Ginny's blood-spattered collar, on which some white hair was stuck, which looked the whiter against the sticky red.

She did not stop by me or look back. I, too, did not call out to her. Had it been some other day I'd have run after her. That afternoon as I sat there alone, I felt the summer had ended; there was little point in going beyond that.

Four

The days grew shorter, the colour of the mountains duller. The sky would be overcast by midday. Darkness gathered much before night fell. In October the sun sheds light as do trees their leaves in autumn. The wilted light withdrew towards the peaks, while a diffuse, pasty glow lingered over the town on the hillside.

Kaya would be out the whole day. With Lama gone, the house appeared desolate. Mother hardly ever stepped out of her bedroom now. She'd grown so ungainly, so blown up, that Kaya couldn't bear to see her. Her mother began to look like another woman, her face the only feature that Kaya felt was still recognizable. It was almost as though Kaya shared the home with a stranger.

Even after Kaya returned at dusk, she would continue to loiter outside the gate. In the twilight the house looked curiously unfamiliar: a two-storey wooden villa, Mrs Joshua's windows closed on the empty veranda on the ground floor, the sloping red tin roof, a black chimney sticking out — this was her home. Babu's room remained bolted. Lama's doors banged whenever the wind rose.

In the evening hush, the rattling doors made the house appear deserted, like the others in town whose owners went away in winter. As Kaya stood on the street a terrifying thought gripped her, that if she turned her back on the house this moment and walked away, no one would call after her; she'd not be missed even if she chose to linger outside all night: the house would remain as unconcerned as those all-seeing mountains. For the first time, then, Kaya came face to face with her loneliness; she saw it all too clearly in the darkness.

Kaya did not fear the loneliness; she was just a little mystified, as though it grew within one like a sickness, out of sight of people — of Chhote, of Mother, of Mrs Joshua. She was growing up unnoticed, unlike Mother, whom everyone noticed.

As Kaya neared her home one evening she was surprised to see the house, except the veranda, in a blaze of lights. This had never happened before. Shadows moved across the lighted window-panes. She knew of no one who might call this late. Mrs Joshua's door too stood wide open, which was very unusual.

Kaya started up the stairs. As soon as she reached the veranda, she saw Bholu, his wobbly head huddled against the trellis. He used to come with Dai Ma the midwife, but never entered a room; Mangtu put out a burlap sack for him to sit on. Small, bronzed, shaven-headed, he looked like an undersized friar.

Kaya knelt beside him.

'How long have you been here, Bholu? When did you come?'

There was a faint flick of his head, his eyelids lifted, his lips parted as in a smile — this was all the answer Bholu was capable of. Kaya couldn't recall when last she'd heard him utter an entire tangible word: what fell from his lips would be a shapeless raw lump, as it were — in a note that was more an echo of an inner silence than a vehicle of meaning. He'd keep humming though, a sort of litany in monotone. His presence here tonight indicated that Dai Ma must be somewhere inside; she always left him to wait on the veranda. Kaya could never quite make out whether it was Bholu who insisted on accompanying Dai Ma or Dai Ma who took him along wherever she went in order to protect him from the world at large.

Kaya sat across from Bholu on the floor. Even though he could not speak, his mere presence in the flitting shadows was reassuring; there was no need for words. Kaya felt as safe with him as she had with Ginny a long time ago. The memory sent a shiver through her.

'Bholu! Bholu!' Kaya chanted to herself, as if to ask him if he, in the silence of his soul, possessed some key to safety that words lacked. But Bholu could hear her no better than Ginny did. He stared at her impassively before his head started to nod again to his out-of-tune humming, his voice thin and piping as a six-month-old's.

The pressure of a hand on Kaya's shoulder roused her. She turned to see Chhote, his breath hot near her throat. She stood up.

'What's it, Chhote?'

'Look', he hesitated. 'Won't you come in?'

Kaya considered him silently. These days Chhote was mostly on his own; they saw each other only at night. Lying in their beds, they would listen to the tattoo of the wind on Lama's door.

'When did Dai Ma arrive?'

'In the afternoon, when you were out.'

Kaya wanted to ask him about Mother, but an unknown fear held her back. She fell in quietly behind Chhote.

As they went by Mother's room, past Babu's closed door, Kaya stole a look inside. She glimpsed Mrs Joshua in a chair by the brazier, Dai Ma on the planking, Mother — her face out of sight — in bed. Kaya did not remember ever having seen Mrs Joshua on the upper floor before; she wondered how the old woman could have climbed up the stairs.

Kaya would always remember this chilly autumn night; it would still be with her years hence — an old photograph, the images blurred, the colours faded, yet evocative: Bholu on the veranda, Mother in her bed, Dai Ma and Mrs Joshua bent forward over the flaming coal in the brazier. It was the first cold night of the autumn, and Mangtu had put coal-burners in the rooms.

Kaya switched on the light in her room. It looked rather empty with her and Chhote's schoolbooks put away in a bundle under the desk, where Ginny used to deposit her spoils. On the wall above, Chhote had stuck a guidebook picture of the town; it showed the Jakhu temple covered in snow, the spire of the church on the Ridge, the Lower Bazar below, and, above all, a red spot which Chhote believed was his school. It was surprising that the picture, threatened all the time by gusts of wind from the side window, had managed to hold out.

Tonight the wind had died down. Even the tin roof did not

clang and clamour with scampering twigs and leaves. The trees in Mrs Joshua's garden stood still. Kaya lay back on her pillow.

'How did Mrs Joshua manage to come up?'

'Mangtu helped her', Chhote said. 'Where were you the whole day? I looked for you everywhere.'

'By the railway line.' Kaya looked hard at Chhote, who stood near her bed.

'Why don't you sit down?'

Somehow Kaya couldn't bear him standing over her; she felt, however irrationally, that if only he got out of the way, her dreary day too would get off her back.

Outside in the autumn mist the trees looked like one another's shadows. A delicate mantle stretched from the eaves to the mountains beyond. The mist must hang over the railway line too, Kaya thought; strange that one couldn't see blood in darkness.

In the veranda, Bholu's singsong rose and fell in an uninterrupted, monotonous rhythm, rather like the drone of a gadfly on a glass pane.

'Chhote, have you ever seen someone dying?'

In the soothing heat from the brazier, Chhote blinked open his sleepy eyes. Why, yes — a number of times: the stiffened birds in the bushes, the carcasses of dogs, ants curled up on clay, moles and earthworms floating in swollen streams. But it was death, not dying; perhaps not even death, for it was something that followed death: a shell that seemed to have had nothing to do with either living or dying. And then Chhote remembered what Mrs Joshua had once told him — that she'd be in the Sanjauli cemetery in another year or two. The earth below, a stone above, which would bear her name, the same as on her letter-box. But for Chhote, even this was not 'dying'; it was simply going off to another place — as the whole neighbourhood did in winter.

'Have you gone to sleep?'

Chhote saw Kaya lying still, sprawled on her bed, eyes closed, unkempt dusty hair over her brow.

Kaya woke up with a start — she was in her own room: Mother must be in hers, Mangtu in the kitchen: by this hour all had repaired to their safe corners. But for Kaya there was no safety, for there was so much going on around her. She could not shut herself in as Lama would; even otherwise, the latch on the door behind which one could hide was too high for her to reach, far beyond her age; if she tried to stretch out for the latch she would only end up hurting her fingers.

'Have *you* seen it, Kaya?'

Kaya sat up in bed.

'What?'

'Death', said Chhote.

'No, I haven't, either', Kaya admitted calmly. 'But I once heard it come.'

'When was it?'

'There's nothing much to it really', said Kaya, engrossed, back again on the track of the distant afternoon. 'I was standing some way from the railway line. The bushes on the other side were swaying. Suddenly then, I heard a call; it seemed to me that someone was calling.'

'Did you see anyone?'

'No, I saw no one. There was just that sound from the tunnel. Ginny was sitting beside the line.' She listened to the call and then she . . . died.

Nothing more to it. Had Lama not called to Ginny, nothing would have happened. Ginny sat stupefied by the track, bound to Lama's voice from across the tunnel, unable to decide whether to go on ahead or crawl back. . . . In that instant, while Kaya sat in bed facing Chhote, it struck her that Ginny was not dead, she had only been called away.

Who had called? Was it Lama, or someone she couldn't see?

Kaya rose to her feet and opened the door slowly. The moon over the chestnut tree shone through the mist like a wick-flame. The washing looped by Mangtu over the trellis to dry stood out sharply. A sheer web of moonlight enveloped the town.

A strange sense of suffocation seized Kaya. She stepped out.

Bholu was in the veranda pacing back and forth, emitting a curious rumbling sound that fell away into an abyss of darkness.

'Does he keep awake all night?' Chhote had followed Kaya out. He was afraid of Bholu, and preferred to keep away from him.

'He'll be all right', said Kaya, buffeted by an unknown emotion, part fear, part protectiveness, amorphous, centred on no one.

'Kaya, doesn't he frighten you?'

'Why should he?'

'When you're together, doesn't he say anything to you?'

'He doesn't say anything to anybody.'

'He does. Can't you hear?'

Bholu was coming round again towards the trellis. His voice rose and fell in the air. But the air did not resound with it, nor retain any mark or trace of it: no remnant, no evidence, as if that sound had a completeness beyond question, a finality of its own. It struck Kaya that a call must be similar — only the creature called could understand it, just as Ginny alone heard the call that afternoon on the railway line.

Was Bholu calling? Or was someone else there besides Bholu, besides the spectral moonlight, on the deserted veranda?

Something happened then which Kaya could not comprehend. Bholu stopped in his tracks, turning round towards where Kaya was, where he had no business to be going, but where perhaps he had to go. He paused opposite her; they could listen to each other's breathing. He reached out a fumbling hand. Kaya stood stock-still as his fingers brushed past her cheeks, groped, caressed, devoid of a sense of direction, numb, almost lifeless they yet moved, explored, tracing the ridge of her dusty eyebrows, the locks of tousled hair over her forehead, the length of forehead — and then it occurred to Kaya that she was feeling her wounds through his fingers, as if the tears bathing her face, washing off the restlessness and misery of the days gone by, had sprung not from her eyes but his blind fingertips . . .

Bholu drew back. Perhaps tears have a memory of their own and awakened something in him. He had strayed for a moment: in his world identities, being illusive, were misleading. He turned about abruptly, the humming that had ceased for the time being already surging, as across an endless desert.

✳

Chhote was not there when Kaya turned back. She smiled to herself, he made himself scarce at the very sight of Bholu! Why did anyone have to be at all afraid of him? One might fear other people, for most are animals in the guise of man, as Lama used to say. But Bholu wore no disguise; he was still a child though older than one, a long way off from the world of both men and animals. She could touch him as she would the trees that basked in their aloneness.

Kaya's tears had dried by now. She marvelled that the night had suddenly grown so luminous. Or perhaps she only thought it had, for nothing in fact had changed — not the trees, not the lights, not the darkness. Only the eyes in her tear-stained face still had a wet sheen.

Kaya felt relieved, beyond hurt, pain, memories. She stood on the veranda overlooked by the moonlit peaks. In the shimmering mist the trees in Mrs Joshua's yard seemed to stretch out their white, bare arms to her.

As white as her mother's, mused Kaya. Her mother had summoned her to her bedroom the other day. The first thing that Kaya noticed on entering were her arms upon the quilt — white and thin, so thin it gave Kaya quite a turn: she thought her mother's bangles would slip off on to the floor. But nothing of the sort happened; the bangles hung in mid-air like everything else about Mother.

'Come here.' Her mother made her sit near her on the bed. 'You're away the whole day — where do you go?' She looked uncertainly at Kaya.

'Nowhere', said Kaya offhandedly: Mother's worries often left her cold.

'Is it true that you spend your day near the railway line?'

'Who told you?'

Kaya's mother stared at her. For a moment she could hardly believe that this girl by her side was her own daughter — pale-looking, large hungry eyes, a hint of fuzz on her chapped top lip, stringy hair all over her forehead. She was visibly upset.

'Kaya,' she raised her eyes, 'it must be lonely for you, with Lama gone, Babu away, I in bed . . .' Her mother trailed off, sighing forlornly.

'You'll soon be well again, won't you?' said Kaya hopefully.

'Don't worry, Kaya — this is not a sickness.'

Kaya eyed her mother suspiciously: she was all bloated up — what was that if not sickness? Nevertheless, she was slightly encouraged, for this was the first time that Mother had spoken to her about herself.

'I forgot to tell you,' her mother went on, 'there's a letter from Bua. She should be here in another day or two.' A gentle smile lit her frail face. 'I thought, when Bua comes this time, you could shift to Chacha's house — what will you do here by yourself?'

Kaya's heart beat fast. To her, Chacha's house seemed more a dream than real. Even though she visited the house only once or twice a year, she would be full of it for months afterwards — of memories of Chacha's library, of her cousin Beeru, of his room. That secluded house atop the hill seemed like a magical palace — above the town, nestling in the clouds.

'Will Bua be staying there?'

'Only for a day. But you can stay on until Babu comes back from Delhi. Then you can come home together.'

'And you?'

'What about me?' her mother asked, surprised.

'Won't you be left alone?'

'Hardly. Mangtu will be here. So also Bua, at least for some days.' Her mother seemed to hesitate for a while. 'Besides, I'll be all right before long.'

The mother regarded Kaya quietly, troubled by a vague ache, a bleakness in her heart: the girl had almost become a stranger who happened to have taken refuge here — and she could do little about it.

Some people are forever beyond help, and her daughter was such a person.

'Look,' the mother ran her fingers through Kaya's hair, 'you don't have to go unless you want to, you understand?'

Kaya shook her head impatiently.

'I'd like to go, but . . .' Kaya stopped, suddenly assailed by a terrible doubt. 'Babu will come there, won't he, to bring me back?'

'Why should I lie to you?' her mother said in an injured tone.

It might not be a lie; still, there was room for doubt. It struck Kaya that her mother only wanted her out of the way, that she was keen on getting rid of her. Kaya told herself she'd tell Mother she wouldn't go anywhere. . . . Then Kaya recalled the last winter; Lama's deserted room loomed in the darkness; the nightmare of Ginny on the railway track returned. *I did nothing amidst all this. Things happened, but these fell by the wayside among the rocks, the leaves, the broken twigs; I didn't even want to look at them. Sometimes, on a quiet afternoon or before going to bed in the night, these started hovering over me — some dreadful fear, a startling sound, a sobbing memory: and I felt that all this had happened in a previous birth — when Lama was here, when Babu had returned to Delhi, when I'd gone to Falkland with Bua: all the things put aside as I went along now filed past me, staring me in the face and I would open this teeming basket of memories and extract them one by one — this happened last winter, and this the winter before — and I allowed myself to be led back to a flickering light of the past where time and happiness and pain were still undefined, where there was no memory, where everything miraculously returned to its pristine condition — light into light, darkness into darkness . . . where light and darkness were nevertheless merged, both dark and alight at the same time, as often happens in the mountains in autumn. But I cannot linger there; I'm in a desperate hurry to get back — to Chhote, to Mangtu in the kitchen, to this house in which I wait for Babu day in, day out.*

Kaya did not go to see her mother after that night; she felt as though Mother was under siege. The light in her room burned round the clock. Mangtu did not spend the nights in his room; he slept instead in the kitchen. Dai Ma, who tended Mother in her room, looked like an aged nurse from a hospital. Bandages, a basin of boiling-hot water, and a sweetish odour filled the room.

Kaya and Chhote kept to themselves. They didn't know who came in or went out. Alone in their room, they deduced from the tread on the stairs that Mangtu was going down, or, by the beat of a walking-stick across the veranda below, that Mrs Joshua was coming up. They rarely heard any other sounds.

But one day there was a stir outside. They both rushed out to the veranda, where Kaya stopped short, amazed. Bua, who used to lose her temper at the mention of a rickshaw, was now noisily heaving herself off a rickshaw seat, her customary bundle in her hands. Those dark spindly legs could only have belonged to her, as also that drawn, exhausted face; it almost seemed she had travelled all the way from Meerut to the hills in that rickshaw. Bua paused to eye Kaya once she struggled up the stairs to the veranda.

'How is your mother?' she asked.

But Bua didn't wait for an answer; she proceeded forthwith towards Mother's room.

'Lama hasn't come!' Chhote voiced his and Kaya's disappointment. When they saw Bua alighting from the rickshaw there had been a sudden quickening of hope in their hearts; they expected Lama to show up behind Bua or the coolies, her dupatta tied round her waist, hair tumbling over her forehead, her shoulders drawn up straight. Long after the rickshaw left, they continued to gaze at the empty afternoon street leading to a seemingly empty bazar.

They hadn't given up waiting for Lama. Crouching by the fire during long winter evenings, they couldn't help thinking of her; they expected her to walk in any minute, quietly, like a wild animal drawn to the warmth, drawing the others to her own warmth even without calling them. The children would look at the veranda every now and then, but Lama's room was in darkness. Kaya shuddered at the slightest noise made by the door and Chhote would shift closer to her. The clothes left on the trellis to dry fluttered in the wind.

The wind had again struck up that night.

'Did you hear?' Chhote asked, frightened.

'There's nothing. Just the clothes. A wind is blowing.'

'Not that, Kaya. There was a sound from Mother's room.'

What sound? Mother's room was at the further end. They saw Dai Ma's shadow on the veranda as she went into the kitchen to speak to Mangtu before going back to Mother in a moment. She had been with Mother the whole afternoon. Something was going on in that room which those grown-ups were keeping from the two of them.

'Is Mother unconscious?'

'Why should she be?' Kaya glared at Chhote. She swept up to where he sat hunched by the door, pulled him to his feet, and dragged him over to his bed. 'Now go to sleep — or I'll go downstairs to talk to Bholu!'

Bholu was in Mangtu's quarters. Occasionally when Dai Ma stayed overnight, Bholu would sleep in Mangtu's room. Chhote crawled into bed without making a fuss, lest Kaya carry out her threat. Had it been some other day, he'd have immediately gone off to Mother if bullied thus — as he did on the nights when he woke up to find Kaya missing from the next bed.

'Kaya! O Kaya!' It was Mangtu calling from the head of the stairs.

Kaya rushed out to where he stood holding Mrs Joshua by her hand.

'Look, Kaya, I've work in the kitchen. Can you help the Memsahib go downstairs?'

Mrs Joshua was groping for the top step with her walking-stick.

Kaya took her hand. Mrs Joshua seemed to have misgivings about the girl.

'After you', said Mrs Joshua. 'And look, my hand isn't made of steel! Don't grip it so hard.'

They descended the stairs, Kaya one step in front.

There was dust on the stairs. Kaya blinked, the wind was in her eyes. Mrs Joshua leaned against the wall for support; she was short of breath, though not short on talk.

'Isn't your father coming?'

'Why, Mrs Joshua — he won't be here until December.'

'But at a time like this . . .' Mrs Joshua hurtled down several steps as if in a fit of anger.

'Doesn't he know?' Mrs Joshua persevered. They were on the ground floor now.

'Know what, Mrs Joshua?' Kaya was perplexed.

Mrs Joshua gave her an annoyed, impatient look. Was Kaya putting it on, or did she really not understand?

Mrs Joshua withdrew her hand from Kaya's.

'I'll manage', she told Kaya, still in a huff.

Nevertheless, Kaya fell in step beside her. It was a moonlit night with deep shadows under the trees. Kaya knew Mrs Joshua would not be able to make it to her flat on her own. Even otherwise, there was a strong wind which forced her eyes half-shut. They kept close to the flower-beds along the wall. The Annandale ground below, and Jakhu Peak above — both were clearly visible from Mrs Joshua's garden. The tin letter-box nailed to the gate rattled in the wind.

'Would you like to come in?' Mrs Joshua said at her door, her voice subdued and gentle, as though she was ashamed of having displayed her temper. 'I'm going to make myself some tea, but you can have an Ovaltine.'

Kaya didn't care for the taste of Mrs Joshua's Ovaltine, but she liked its smell — and so for a moment she was tempted. Then it crossed her mind that Chhote must be missing her.

'Some other time, Mrs Joshua, thank you.'

'Will you be going to Falkland?'

Kaya nodded.

'Tell your uncle I'm still alive.' Mrs Joshua laughed softly, and turned away.

Kaya stared after her. In the moonlight Mrs Joshua's laughter sounded strangely sinister. Kaya waited until Mrs Joshua opened the door of her unlit flat and went in.

Kaya woke up in the middle of the night. She had turned off the lamp before going to sleep, but the moonlight glancing off the balcony picked out Chhote in his bed as well as the picture on the wall above the writing desk and the bundles of books underneath.

Something was afoot, she told herself. There was something in the air which had woken her.

She got out of bed and opened the door. Shadows on the wall moved with the trees across the veranda ablaze with moonlight. Silence reigned in the drawing room but muffled voices seeped through from Mother's bedroom across it. The light in the kitchen was still on.

As soon as Kaya came out to the moonlit veranda she realized she was a sitting duck, that she could be easily spotted and sent back to her room. There were no dark corners near at hand where she could have hidden herself.

Kaya went back to the room and then crossed over to the bathroom. The service door opened into the gallery which was fastened around the back of the house like a belt. The house was sandwiched between the veranda in front and the passageway behind. Whenever Kaya wanted to slip away to Mangtu's rooms she took this passage down to her 'secret' flight of stairs which led to the backyard. Mrs Joshua never came out to this part of the yard because of the refuse heap there. Between the house and Mangtu's rooms stood the chestnut tree. Its branches, laden with chestnuts, overhung the outbuilding on the one hand and the eaves of the double-storeyed house on the other. When a rising wind woke Kaya at night, she listened in the darkness to the playful jostling of the branches against the tin roof.

Kaya waited just outside the service door. The night was not very cold but the wind set her nerves tingling. She recalled another night from the previous winter when she had sat crosslegged here, stark-naked, praying fervently to Kali Ma. As the memory flooded back, her body went rigid and her skin prickled.

Kaya finally turned into the passage, creeping along, her heart almost failing her. She knocked against a bucket or a phenyl bottle and froze, expecting the entire household — Mangtu, Bua, everybody — to descend upon her in a rush. She trembled in fear. Then she took another step, and yet another, until she found herself looking into the sitting room. Her gaze held to the billowy matting, which Chhote variously called his swimming pool or lake. Indeed, among the chairs and tables and almirahs, in the moonlight it did look like a rippling, choppy lake.

Kaya's hands stuck as if glued to the glass pane she was gazing through when she heard an uncanny sound, not a scream, but a raw trumpeting, razor-sharp, smothered in another instant into a throaty rattle. Was Mother making the sound? That was hard to believe; it couldn't be a human cry. Kaya ran up to the window of her mother's bedroom. She pushed hard at it, palms flattened

against the panes, fingertips white from the pressure and cold —
but couldn't open it: the window was bolted from inside. No
one heard her. She took a hold on herself and tried to locate that
burst of sound, that scream which a moment ago had rent the
air keen-edged as a knife. She peered in; one end of the curtain
was stuck some way up the bottom pane. The room beyond was
filled with light, but she could see only a patch not much larger
than her palm — the size of the spot that misted under her warm
breath. She wiped the mist off with her spittle, bending her eye
to the cleaned spot to see what was going on inside.

Three empty chairs lay around a brazier. Glowing embers lit
the red-patterned flowers of the wallpaper. Kaya could see the
foot of the bed and Mother's legs on it. So many times while
playing on the gallery, Kaya had looked through this window at
Mother surrounded by her things, yet aloof, ageless, a white doll
of wax — the focus of Kaya's feelings no matter where she
wandered. Had she ever imagined then that the memories of her
mother scattered all round would one day come together on a
bed in a benumbing blur of naked legs parted below a torso like
the trunk of a felled tree, which she would see from outside,
through a window in the darkness?

Kaya was surprised that she had not been caught yet, shooed
or borne away. She was free even as she clung to the window.
She was standing out in the open. The wind blew up her bare
legs, from the cracks in the timber flooring, hammering nails
into her goose-pimples. Her grip on the window jambs tightening, she shrank into herself as a shadow went past.

Nothing happened, though; no one noticed Kaya. She cleaned
another spot on the pane, and saw Dai Ma at her mother's bedside
with a bowl of steaming hot water in her hands. Bua spoke to
her briefly, but Kaya only saw her lips move. Bua took the bowl
from Dai Ma and put it under the bed. She looked as unflappable
as when holding her own against the rickshaw-pullers.

And then Kaya heard the scream again. She wrenched her
head around, unable to take the sheer violence of it. At first she
was too shocked to be certain whether the sound had come
from within the room. She looked out over the rustling trees,
into the quiet night, at the hills drenched in moonlight. It

seemed impossible to Kaya that the piercing scream which had cut her through and through had left the mountains unmoved. The scream was made all the more terrifying by the apathy of the very mountains that Kaya had learned to look upon as her kin: to think that they should now stand apart as total strangers! Unconcerned, indifferent, cool — as if they had never had anything to do with her. Clad in mist and moonlight, they maintained a glacial aloofness. Kaya shivered involuntarily, turning towards the window again.

Bare white legs parted wide — like a pair of scissors. Did these belong to Mother? Kaya pressed her burning cheeks against the chill glass. Mother's face was hidden behind Dai Ma; her trunk stuck out unabashed and naked. A nest of veins on it leaped into view now and then. Kaya could not trust her eyes: her own eyes seemed to be playing tricks on her. That was Mother's leg, surely? And that arm jutting out as if from the wrong end — was that hers too? Mother was a tangle of arms and legs, like a doll whose limbs have got mixed up in play.

It wasn't merely that something was happening to Mother — it was that something was being done to her.

The kitchen door creaked open. Alarmed, Kaya made to pull away from the window but was relieved to see a preoccupied Mangtu move straight towards Dai Ma — without a glance in the direction of the bed. He looked gigantic beside Bua and Dai Ma. His pigtails flowed from under the topi on his head in the manner of the unruly locks of Tibetan mendicants. He laid cotton-wool and rags torn from old saris on the edge of the bed.

I must turn back, Kaya told herself — back to my own room, to Chhote. But her hands on the glass pane refused to comply, as though they were independent of her, mere shadows of Mother's raised hands on the bed. She willed her hands to draw back, and at that moment a hand on the bed flung out violently — gold bangles gleaming — as if trying to rid itself of that blue spider of veins. Kaya had never witnessed such complete pain before. She watched spellbound, awe-struck, as that quivering body writhed like a worm under a rock. Each wave bore Mother deeper into a dungeon of pain. Only Dai Ma's hands crawled forward between Mother's thighs, clutching in her wizard hands

Mother's arched body. . . . *No! No!* Kaya cried, her nails clawing the sheet of glass, her dry, chapped, trembling lips chafing against the window-frame. The sooty wood-varnish tasted bitter and metallic on her tongue. Kaya sank to her feet where a bar of light from the window lay inert in the ghostly pallor of the moon . . . and she began to dream. She dreamed that Mother was somewhere there in the breezy shadows. Had this also happened a long time ago when Kaya was still a child, when memory was not yet hitched to time — in a previous birth? She thought she could see again a frightened little girl, crying, full of a foreboding, stumbling across a vast stretch towards her mother sunning herself under the chestnut tree, who at once gathered her in her arms.

Five

Kaya did not realize how long she'd been sitting on the gallery, huddled for warmth, beyond sleep, gathering in the wandering wind, the clanging tin roof, the rustling chestnut tree. It was quiet now in Mother's bedroom. Kaya thought she'd wait until the light was turned off — in another ten minutes, perhaps — before tiptoeing in the darkness back to her room. No one would ever know that she had not been in bed that night.

Then Kaya heard it again — the scream; sharp as jagged glass, it gored her soul. She sprang to her feet and threw herself at the window: Mother's legs a pair of scissors, wide apart, with Dai Ma leaning over them. Then Kaya collapsed in a heap like an empty gunny sack, on the split, creaking floorboards. 'Kaya, is that you? What are you doing up here so late?' Mangtu tipped up her face. He shook her by her shoulders even as she swayed like a drunk. 'Don't you have any sense of shame, Kaya?' Kaya stared at him. Shame — she'd heard that word before, many times, but it never had anything to do with her. Even the world between Mother's open legs — her naked body racked by spasms — was above shame, chaste, pure.

Mangtu swept Kaya up in his arms, as he used to do years earlier when she was a baby. But as he started to walk, she seemed to come awake. She flailed her legs like an epileptic. 'No, no! I'll not go to my room!' she cried. A storm broke within her. The hills in the darkness beyond swam round with her shrieks. 'You stupid girl, can't you see we're not going to your room?' Mangtu held her ankles in an unyielding grip. The wooden slats shook under him. He began to descend the stairs to the backyard and

Kaya calmed down, her muscles relaxed: Mangtu was taking her to his room. Reassured, she clung to him; she felt safe; every step that Mangtu took brought her nearer her place of refuge.

The 'servants' quarters' or 'outhouses' adjoined the main houses; single rooms black with soot, these had burlap curtains for doors. The flapping burlap soothed her on solitary winter afternoons. Before long, however, she would grow unaware of it, as those on a ship do of ocean sounds. She often lay there contented in the half-light, surrounded by bedbugs and the musty smell of damp, decaying wood — until the crickets created an uproar. Their stridulous wings poked and stirred the silence, letting it flow in. Kaya would wrap Mangtu's blanket closely about her. 'Stop! Don't come in!' she commanded. 'It's me here.' She would shrink into herself, into the furthest nook of her being, where scrawled as on a wall was her name, *Kaya*. 'Look, it's I! Kaya!' At the mention of her name, the silence retreated behind the burlap curtain, whereupon the crickets raised another rumpus.

This was one place no one else in the household knew anything about. Not even Lama, or Chhote — not because Kaya wanted to keep it a secret but simply because she was herself ignorant of the secret that drew her to Mangtu's. She was alone here. At night everyone retired to their rooms after dinner. Kaya, too, accompanied Chhote to their room, changed into night-clothes and pretended to go to sleep, lying in bed on her stomach, breathing deeply, evenly. When Chhote fell asleep something obscure and forbidden beckoned her. An insane mist roamed the mountains beyond her window, as if the sleep in her eyes was roaming in the mist and had lost its way. She would sit up, wear a pullover over her night-dress, and slip out along the gallery to the backyard below. Outside, she would raise a worried head for a breath of fresh air — and see the familiar patch of sky between Mangtu's room and the two chimneys of the house.

And her breath would catch. Kaya would find herself standing in the no man's land of Mrs Joshua's garden — an island of darkness from which the birch trees reared. Moonlight broke into spangles on their leaves. She'd heard that Mrs Joshua had planted these trees herself when she came here as a young woman. The trees and Mrs Joshua had grown old together. Kaya's heart throbbed louder as she guided her steps through deep shadows under the trees, for fear that Mrs Joshua might overhear the roar of her blood and emerge to call her back. She held her fist over her chest and broke into a run, past the moaning trees and towards the small bridge slung between two bamboo poles.

'I've made it', Kaya would say to herself. 'You keep talking to yourself', Chhote used to grumble. He was in bed now and will reach out in his sleep towards my empty bed, thought Kaya; his hands will beat the air between the two beds; he'll start and wake up, and find me gone. Wasn't this, too, a kind of pain? Kaya would grip the poles on either side of the narrow bridge; she wanted to hold on to something solid in that darkness, as if seeking the strength to admit to herself *that this was pain, this was me, this was fear.* The moon would have risen above the trees. Between the bushes, the khud shone like a golden hair-parting. There was a tight little hissing blast of wind, which on quiet nights broke into sobs. Kaya would be hard-put to tell where those sobs came from — from the bushes, or the scraping of the leaves of trees . . . or could it be that they arose from within her?

Kaya would shiver in the cold, and hug herself, turning around to look again at the house. Those two chimneys and the chestnut tree seemed to have drawn apart: the house that linked them had itself almost disappeared in the darkness. But the light in the kitchen would still be on. Mangtu had yet to wash the dishes and swab the kitchen floor. Then, he'd do his nightly rounds of the house, lantern in hand . . . Kaya would lie on the floor of Mangtu's room, facing away from the wall, tugging at her pullover as if it were a blanket. Was it strange, she thought, that she preferred to be in Mangtu's room rather than her own? She wanted others to notice how lonely she was. Sometimes though, she merely lingered in the doorway, the burlap curtain drawn aside. No, she wasn't really alone: there were all those lights dotting the hillside — and where there were lights there must be people. And like her, they must still be up. She wondered if people among the lights could see her, the way she could see them, through the wind and darkness. Her skin tingled at the thought of another person's eyes on her. It filled her with a vague melancholy; but also a sense of affinity would spread through her — the sort that makes a bird in the all-pervasive silence of the forest cry out in response to the call of another of its kind. She would rock back and forth as waves of sleep swept over her. At the back of her mind a thought flickered, as if coming across the mist, that Mangtu would soon be here. She tried to keep sleep at bay till he arrived.

But tonight she was wide awake — stunned and speechless. Eyes staring, she sat hunched where Mangtu had left her. Only a moment ago she had been screaming her head off, kicking, thrashing her arms about, as Mangtu carried her downstairs. But the moment he sat her on the floor in his room and turned to go back, she was struck dumb — like a ham actor who shouts and shrieks, gesticulating wildly, throwing about arms and legs on the stage, only to slump emptily as soon as the curtain falls. *I stood at the window. I saw the room flooded with light, Dai Ma carrying a steaming hot-water bowl, Mother — a leaping, dipping flame of pain on her curled fingertips — clawing at the steam, clutching, letting go.* Kaya felt this was continuing, it had not ended — in the darkness she would keep clinging all her life to the window, looking in at the relentless dance of the flame.

She started and sat up. Drenched in sweat, she shed Mangtu's blanket and her pullover. The wind had abated. A pale sliver of moonlight crept in round the burlap curtain. Kaya heard the lilt of a low voice behind the side wall. It floated up like a puff of smoke, eddying, chasing its own tail.

Kaya stealthily went out. Mist drifted from the terraced fields at the foothills to halfway up the mountainside. But Kaya ignored it, and her own shadow that lurched up the chestnut tree. She turned into the gallery, from which two steps down another door led to an empty room where occasionally Bholu slept at night when Dai Ma was delayed.

Kaya was beyond fear tonight. She had outgrown childhood ways of tracing the lines of fear and then dodging them haltingly. Everything was dwarfed by what she'd recently seen from the window. Pain diminishes grown-ups, but it had made her grow up. So as she now stood in the doorway looking a little more closely at Bholu than before she realized that he was, after all, no different from others.

He was humming.

Kaya stepped in over the threshold. A paraffin lamp glimmered in the middle of the room and seemed to sway the sooty beam above. Bholu's head swayed, too — up and down, down and up, ceaselessly. 'See, Bholu, it's me. I'm Kaya, whose cheeks you touched.' Her lips twitched. She was standing between the lantern and Bholu, his head lowered, unseeing eyes turned up, his mouth a dark gaping hole. Perhaps Kaya was no more to him than a flea he could extract from his eyes with a mere flutter of his lashes. There was no trace of recognition in Bholu's eyes. He didn't even seem to remember that this was the girl whose tears had wet his fingertips not long ago. For Bholu no incident was related to another, there was no sense of continuity, for he was outside time — like a child for whom the moment in hand is complete in itself, for whom every pain is final with no escape route, no relief or redress.

'I heard you singing, so I came over', said Kaya. 'I was in the next room.' Her words tried to traverse vast stretches of desert. She hoped Bholu might dredge from his memory some inkling of what was beyond words. Bholu's head jerked like that of a mechanical puppet giving a last nod or two as it finally winds down. He paused a moment before his hand went up, as if to draw out with index and middle fingers his voice that seemed stuck in his throat like a sparrow trapped in a thicket; the guttural monosyllables that he retrieved were unintelligible by themselves, yet they appeared to grapple with some kind of meaning.

Kaya walked past the lantern to where Bholu's shadow splayed out from the wall on to the floor. Warmth swept through her. Her sorrows, like bits of straw, lined the eyrie in which she wrapped herself. Beyond the door was the moonlight on the mountains and the noisy rustle of bushes along the narrow-gauge railway track. Kaya put all this behind her and entered the mute, timeless world of Dai Ma's son. His mouth hung open and showed his white, jutting teeth. Flawless, like Ginny's — that splash of pure white as Ginny opened her mouth one last time between the rails, her tail beating in fear, minutes before she

died. *Look, you could have saved Ginny, couldn't you?* She heard
Lama's laughter among the bushes. . . . *You crazy, stupid girl! See,
that's your Ginny there, fur caked with dark blood, another tuft blowing
away along the track like candyfloss.*

Kaya looked around — there was little to see, but she saw
Bholu gaping at her. In that instant a radiant, wondrous happiness surged through her and she rode its crest, up, far up,
from where she could see the gravel below, the ballast, Ginny's
body, Mother's limp wide-open legs, clearly — like the remains
of a wayside skeleton in bright daylight which one passed
without a glance or a thought, little realizing that once those
very bones must have been fleshed out with trembling lips
and a throbbing heart. Propelled by this strange, fearsome,
excruciating joy, Kaya took Bholu's hand, eager to share with
him her moment of release — so rare, so elusive. 'Please
Bholu, say something — there's nothing to fear', she whispered.
'Your mother's upstairs with mine. We're alone here, no one
can harass you. Look, Bholu, this is me, *Kaya* — it was your
fingers that touched my face, remember?' Impassive, Bholu
only stared at the workings of her lips. His shaven head reflected
the blue light thrown by the lantern. Suddenly, he flattened
his palms on the floor, as if preparing to get up; but he didn't
budge even an inch. He seemed to gesture towards the door
with his head. Kaya turned around. She saw nothing. Had
Bholu seen something there she couldn't — some longing,
some unknown yearning that hovered in the ghostly light of
an aching, misty night sky?

There was a sudden gust of wind. The horned moon was caught
in branches of the chestnut tree. The tree stirred, another picked
up the cue — and yet another, until the forested hillside began
to hum. Mrs Joshua's letter-box, stuffed with the London papers,
swung open, its small shutters clapping a repetitive rhythm. The
wooden structure of the servants' quarters shook in its frame and
Kaya steadied herself by holding on to the door. The burlap
curtain flapped vigorously in the wind.

'What are you doing here in the doorway?'

Mangtu held Kaya by her shoulders even as she turned to him.

'I thought you had gone to sleep', a weary Mangtu groaned, almost despairing of her. He was weary of the night, of Kaya, of Bholu nodding in the corner.

Mangtu was a big man; from head to toe he looked like an overstuffed, rough-and-ready roll of bedding — with a hand sticking out from one side, an ear from another. But his voice, cool and calm, hung in mid-air as if it did not belong to him or bear any relation to his body.

Mangtu walked past Kaya on his heavy, tired feet. She watched from the doorway; he was like a hunter sneaking upto his un-suspecting quarry. For a moment the two seemed to confront each other. Then Mangtu bent over Bholu, his pigtails swinging over the boy's raised face, and gently removed his hands off the floor, whispering something in his ear. Though Kaya did not hear what Mangtu said, she saw Bholu smile, as if at last some understanding had dawned upon him. Childlike, Bholu obedi-ently let Mangtu take off his clothes until he was left in his vest and shorts. Mangtu made him lie on the pallet bed; he whispered in his ear again and again, more loudly now. But Kaya could not make head or tail of it as she did not understand the hill dialect. For all she knew, he was repeating just one word over and over like a magic formula. Soon Bholu's taut body began to relax like a curled-up snake's in a basket. Mangtu blew off the lantern, and the room plunged into darkness. He took Kaya's hand to lead her away but she shook him off angrily. As she turned her back on Bholu, she could sense his eyes still on her.

'Let's go', Mangtu urged her.

'Where?'

'To your room, of course!'

Kaya went to Mangtu's room instead. Mangtu followed her in.

Kaya knew she was throwing a tantrum, but she could not stop herself; she was, simply, in no mood to go to Chhote yet.

'Could I sleep here, Mangtu?' she said slowly.

Mangtu studied her. He had seen her growing all these years, but could not recollect her as a baby. He had come to look upon her as being one with things eternal — like those trees, those rocks, the mountains, always the same, always present.

'You're frightened, Kaya?' Mangtu stroked her hair.

A cold shiver ran down Kaya's spine. He was so indulgent, so patient, Kaya knew she could trust him. They sat together in silence. No sounds from the adjoining room, not even of breathing. The house was submerged in darkness. Only the light in Mrs Joshua's room was still on — but then, it was on throughout the night, anyway.

'Did you notice Ma was weeping?' Kaya ventured diffidently, trying to gain a foothold among the shards of her mother's things.

'How do you know?' Mangtu fixed his gaze on her.

'I was standing at the window. I saw everything.'

A moan wound through Mangtu's time-worn bones to escape from his lips on to his steaming breath. He sat hunched, rubbing his hands on his knees.

'You saw everything?'

'I told you I was standing at the window.'

'You saw that, too?' Mangtu's hands went dead on his kneecaps.

'I did.' Kaya could still see it all clearly. 'It came up in Dai Ma's hands.' It had emerged from between Mother's thighs — a raw red-and-blue lump of jelly, a nightmare, a beguiling impostor. That thing which had bloated Mother had turned out to be so small, so undignified.

Shhh . . . shh . . . the wind and Mangtu's breath whistled. *Not a single breath*, Kaya grieved silently. Mangtu went back to massaging his knees. *Had it taken but one breath, another would have followed by itself, leading to yet another, and the cycle would have gone on and on.*

Kaya closed her eyes. Breath. She was walking along the railway track, where Ginny lay breathing evenly in the sun. The track seemed endless. It shuddered under the clattering train wheels. It seemed to Kaya that Ginny would be safe as long as she kept walking.

Mangtu stood up. He cracked his fingers one after another. Slowly then he started to unwrap his puttees made of strips torn from Kaya's, Lama's and Chhote's old clothes, which he wore like stockings. Kaya watched with bated breath as the pile on the floor grew larger with each unwinding movement of Mangtu's hand. At last the legs emerged, followed by the chapped heels. Mangtu pressed his fingertips against the roughened soles, as if to squeeze out the ache. He lit a candle. The room seemed to close in as he tipped it, while shadows jumped up on the wall. The molten wax fell in drops from the tongue of the sputtering flame into the red-edged fissures in his coarse skin. 'Ah! Ah!' exclaimed Mangtu, pleasure weaving into the exhalation of ache on his breath. Gradually his sighs were free of both pleasure and pain, and he up-ended the candle. The humped shadows, which looked like hills on the wallscape, returned to the darkness beyond the burlap curtain. 'Did it lessen the pain, Mangtu?' Kaya gazed keenly at his soles. 'Well, not really,' admitted Mangtu slightly dispiritedly, 'it goes for just a while.' Kaya peered under the hardened tallow, into the raw cracks in Mangtu's skin, dark with dirt. The pain had been stopped for now, she consoled herself. Reassured, she stretched out on the floor. Mangtu, too, lay down.

The wind had blown the curtain aside. Kaya stared into the darkness. She had a curious feeling that the range of hills had moved quite close. Near the top of that wooded hill crouched Chacha's villa. The villa was not visible, but on moonlit nights one could see a globe there, the size of a matchstick flame. It was called Falkland — a strange name for a house. She had been on visits there with Mother a number of times in the past. It was far-off, across a deserted wood. Whenever she had asked Mother to take her to Chacha's during the last few months, she just laughed the idea away. She was several months gone; how could she go up the steep hills? But, Kaya had no idea what she meant by saying she was several months gone. Just what did it mean? How could one be gone when one was right here? And as for time, it always went by, didn't it?

'Mangtu', whispered Kaya, not for his benefit but her own: the sound of his name was somehow comforting. He was asleep, but only lightly, as usual. He opened his eyes and asked, 'Who is it? Why, you're still awake, Kaya!'

Kaya was still up, though she was certainly sleepy. She wanted to snuggle against him but a distasteful whiff, which she had not outgrown all these years, put her off. She willed herself to ignore her distaste, and crawled beside him under his blanket. Her feet struck something hard and cold on his feet. 'Mangtu', she mumbled, recoiling. Mangtu snorted. The floorboards creaked under him. The wind blew in through the slats to chill their bones.

'What's that on your ankle?' Kaya drew back her feet, tingling from the icy touch. 'How come you've never noticed them before?' said Mangtu sleepily. 'These are bronze anklets.' So hard, so cold, chafing against the anklebone. 'They must clang', Kaya laughed. 'You always wear puttees over them, so how could I have known?' Mangtu laughed, too, between spasms of coughing. He sat up and looked at Kaya in the half-light as she lay with her hair spread about her. 'I've been wearing them ever since I was a little boy. This is a custom among villagers in the mountains. They put them round the legs of infants . . . and there they remain for the rest of one's life.'

'For the rest of one's life — really? Don't you ever have to change the pair?' Kaya lifted her head. 'Who would? One would have to chop off the feet first.' Kaya snuggled up closer, no longer bothered by the unpleasant smell. 'No, no, I didn't mean that. But don't they fit too tightly when one grows up?' She again moved her feet down to touch his. 'What fit too tightly, Kaya?' Mangtu had drifted off again, losing track of what she had been saying; in that half-light he was doubtful even about the reality of his own being. 'These anklets, what else? What happens when one grows up?' Kaya answered angrily. 'Do these also grow with the feet?' Her voice was pitched so high that Mangtu's sleep retreated before it. 'Have a look at my feet — aren't the anklets just right?' Mangtu's pigtails tumbled over Kaya.

'Do these anklets of bronze grow too — like toe-nails?'

'Well, they've a life of their own, as men do.'

'They do? And then . . .' Kaya's voice trailed off into silence.

'Yes?' Mangtu leaned back against the wall, closing his eyes.

'And what happens when one dies?'

'They shrink.' Mangtu took a deep breath. 'They become as small as when fitted on to the infant. They are not removed even when a man becomes a pile of ashes; they dangle from the burnt bones.'

Kaya moved away and went back to her pallet bed. She felt as if she herself, her body and her legs were separate from one another, that the void among the three was filled with the wind that rushed in through the wooden slats.

Like wind, like breath. There is the inrush of the first breath, then of another, and so the cycle gets underway. . . . Kaya turned on her side. It seemed to her that she was still standing at the window. Two diminutive feet between Mother's raised legs . . . anklets on charred bones, never removed, as small as a newborn's feet, that must clang when the wind rises and blows the ashes about.

Mangtu, didn't it take even a single breath?

Truly, wasn't there even a hint of breath?

Ever so slight a hint?

No?

Six

'How will you go?' asked Chhote.
   'I'll climb up the steps', said Kaya.
   'In that case, I'll go by the path. Will you wait if you reach before me?'

Kaya watched him scamper off. The path rose behind the Kali temple like the curved body of a squirrel. It bore the hoof-marks of ponies and mules. Chhote was trying to land his feet in those marks as he ran.

No one remembers when the two routes to the temple came into being. Walkers used the steps, while the path served ponies and mules. Tall pines soared above the fork, shedding their needles on the stone steps as well as the path.

Chhote kept an eye on Kaya as he trotted up the path. Each time he looked round he saw that she was still sitting where he'd left her. Twice he shouted her name but, even though echoes rolled back from the hills, she did not seem to hear. Then she was gone, the sun glinting white on the deserted, drowsy stone steps.

It was a November afternoon. Both Kaya and Chhote had been at a loose end with their mother bed-ridden and Mangtu busy with his chores about the house. Once Kaya had even gone down to Mrs Joshua's but found the door closed; it seemed it had not been opened for a long time. Her letter-box was still crammed with English periodicals and its shutters clapped as it swung in the wind. When Kaya heard that sound in the brooding silence of night she thought of fretting pigeons seeking flight out of their coop.

Meanwhile, Dai Ma continued to call at least once a week, bringing with her dry fruit, almonds, medicinal herbs, wrapped in a rag. Her son Bholu, left to wait on the veranda, kept repeating an unending, tuneless drone, indifferent to everything around him. He didn't so much as glance at Kaya — or if he did, his eyes held no trace of remembering the evening he had walked up to her and touched her face: if he saw Kaya he seemed not to recognize her, as if she wasn't there at all.

Then one day Mangtu came to Kaya's room unexpectedly. 'Dai Ma wants to see you, Kaya. Hurry up! She's asked after you several times in the last few days.' Surprised, Kaya gaped at him. 'She wants to see me? Are you sure?' Since that fateful night, Kaya had withdrawn into herself. She could hardly believe that anyone would be interested in her — least of all Dai Ma. Dai Ma was a dwarf-like woman, shy and self-centred, and she exuded an aura of mystery and magic, rather like the shimmery web a witch or a sorceress spins around herself in fairy tales. When she came to the house now she would make straight for Mother's bedroom.

This was a recent development, as earlier Dai Ma would always stop and chat if Kaya ran into her on the steps or in the veranda. 'Ah, it's you, Kaya Devi!' she'd exclaim, her dry, scaly lips in a wrinkled face spreading into a broad smile, her gaze held somewhere above Kaya's head as if she was seeing some strange creature there — and she seemed to talk to the creature rather than to Kaya. 'How you've grown, girl! You're already taller than me. You know,' she laughed, 'when I found you in the ravine behind the mountains and brought you here, you were as small as this.' Saying this, Dai Ma would extend her hand — a mere stump, a dried-up twig — that appeared from under the fold of her dupatta covering her chest and abdomen. The hand reminded Kaya of a dried twig and she wondered then if there wasn't a real hand behind that twig which worked it. In such moments she felt that Dai Ma was in fact talking to the invisible creature over her head.

Kaya followed Mangtu out of the room like an automaton. Her home seemed unfamiliar to her. The floorboards creaked under Mangtu's heavy feet. A disquieting suspicion arose within her, for Dai Ma had never ever asked to see her in Mother's room before. Dai Ma had probably spotted her looking in from the window that night, when she saw what she was not expected to. She suspected she was going to be questioned closely, like a witness at a trial. Kaya flinched at the thought, and felt like throwing up. She was seized by the need to flee. Mangtu wouldn't miss her until he looked round, and by then she would be safely out of sight under Chhote's bed, where no one was likely to look for her. Anyway, they would soon give up. People forget easily, she knew — although she herself couldn't forget anything: every little detail of that night was still searingly vivid in her mind.

Kaya didn't flee, but dragged herself along behind Mangtu. Her mother's room was at the far end overlooking what some people still called the Hilta Pahar or Moving Hills — after a young Englishmen of yore who, having picked up some Hindustani, had obviously enjoyed coining new, even if somewhat inappropriate, hybrid words. The tiered hills, densely wooded, were so called because they seemed to move as the thick growth of trees undulated when the wind rose. In winter, though, the trees often did not move at all. The hills would normally come into view as soon as Kaya stepped into Mother's room. But today she saw no hills and wondered for a moment if she'd entered the wrong room. She paused at the door. The window opposite, which revealed the hills, was closed. Mother's bed had been moved under the window, through which just the other night Kaya had watched as Mother, her body contorted, let out piercing cries. The sun now streamed in over a listless Mother huddled at the edge of her bed.

'Come here, girl — don't be afraid.' Dai Ma pulled Kaya in and sat her at the foot of the bed. As it shook, her mother opened her eyes wide. She stared at Kaya speechlessly. Her eyes reflected neither love nor anxiety, just a certain withdrawal, through which she yet seemed to fumble towards Kaya. 'Look,' Dai Ma said in an undertone, 'where do you spend the whole day?' She tapped Kaya under the chin. 'Do you think you could give me the slip?'

Dai Ma chuckled, the fleshy folds of her stomach jiggling merrily while the rest of her — her shoulders, and legs under the green petticoat — remained stock-still. Kaya watched the waves of mirth break on top of her petticoat, thinking of Lama who used to say that Dai Ma had three balls in her abdomen which had weighed her down, which chased one another around her middle in a game of hide-and-seek whenever she laughed. Never having seen Dai Ma naked — just her own mother, Kaya had not quite given those doughy masses of flab a thought, but she had a feeling that if Dai Ma undressed this moment they would at once tumble out and roll away. She looked straight at Dai Ma with open curiosity.

Dai Ma's hand had retreated under the dupatta covering her abdomen. There was now some movement a little above the edge of the petticoat. Soon her groping hand emerged, holding a crimson velvet pouch ornamented with stars of silver thread. Her small hand dipped into the pouch. 'Look here, Kaya, do you know what this is?' She held a string in the palm of her hand. 'This is a string of coral beads', she went on, smiling through the cobwebs of her age. *This is no sorceress, but Dai Ma — giggling, swinging the string in her hand.* 'Here, take it. Don't be afraid — it won't gobble you up. Hold it by the tassel and pass it over your mother's head three times round. Can you count? Ah, that's a really nice, clever girl we have. Now move it downwards — over the shoulders, the throat, the chest, the abdomen, both legs, feet. . . . Make sure you don't miss any part of the body.' As Kaya passed the string of beads all over her, Mother gazed on Kaya with large, unblinking doll's eyes. The sun glinted off the paillettes on the pouch, into her eyes. Dai Ma went on droning like a bumble-bee. Dreamily, Kaya travelled far into the past, into her early terror-stricken childhood — and beyond it, beyond the point of her birth, back to some previous life. The midday sun, the dozing hills, the huddled figure of her mother and, above all, the string swinging from her hand.

'Your mother has come back from the brink.' Dai Ma wrung Kaya's hand. The beads cut into her palm, and a tickling sensation spun through her. 'Your mother has been under the sway of unfavourable stars. These beads have absorbed their evil influence, so now there's nothing to fear any more. Look here, and listen carefully.' Dai Ma paused, unclenching Kaya's fingers. The string, damp with sweat, changed hands; it came to lie coiled like a snake, red tassle-tongue sticking out, in Dai Ma's palm. 'You know the Kali temple, don't you? That's the place where you'd play catch-the-thief with Lama. Don't I know, girl? I know everything.' Dai Ma had her belly-laugh again. There wasn't a single tooth in her cavernous mouth. 'Leave this string at the temple. But take care no one sees you — not even the pujari. Just drop it at the feet of Kali when no one is looking. You understand, little doll?' Dai Ma's pleased chortle was cut short as Mother sat up breathlessly. She reached out a hand to caress her daughter's head. 'Mind doing it? You won't be afraid, no? You can take Chhote along if you like.' She paused before continuing in a distant voice: 'And don't worry, I'll be all right, h'm? I'll not come to any harm.' This was the first time that her mother had spoken to her since that night, the first time that she touched her where tears dwell. Tears now streamed down Kaya's cheeks. Her eyes gazed past Mother, out through the window behind her, to the sun-splashed hills — and for a long, long moment she wasn't certain looking through the spate of her tears whether she herself was quivering or whether it was Hilta Hills that shook.

The coral string was still grasped in Kaya's sticky hand. Chhote eyed her clenched fist from time to time but asked no questions. Had he asked Kaya would have readily opened her fist, told him everything Dai Ma had told her, and dragged him past the fear of the unknown to the feet of Ma Chandika, whose gleaming ebony-black body was often in her thoughts.

Kaya often play-acted. On long, quiet winter afternoons when no one was around to deter her, she would slip out to the passage at the back of the house. Alone, she would close her eyes. The narrow gallery shook in the wind. A hungry fire burned in her dry throat. *Ma Chandika! Kali Ma! Come to me. I wait for you. I can give up everything for your sake, go wherever you bid me to go.* Her lips, parted in a crazed smile, trembled. She believed that the greater the hardships she inflicted on her body, the greater would Kali Ma's appreciation of her be. What started as play-acting then gained the momentum of belief. She would loose hold of herself. A hush seemed to fall within and without her. She would take off her frock, her vest, her salwar. The clothes fell in a heap about her. She opened her eyes slightly and looked at the heap with pride. She shut her eyes again in prayer. *Look, Chandika Ma! I mean what I say. I'm prepared to sacrifice my all. See, I've already cast off everything. I've no one with me. I'm all alone.*

With her clothes off, Kaya was indeed like a derelict — lost and lonely. The wind whistled through the passage, the clothes at her feet fluttered, and her exposed body shook like an aspen. A vague but pleasant thought occurred to her that she would catch cold, go down with pneumonia, and so make an offering of her life to Goddess Kali. Carried away, she started stroking her naked body.

Kaya had a strange feeling that the hands that stroked her were Kali Ma's, not her own. *What a courageous devotee! This little girl, braving the cold, naked.* Kaya's hair flowed down, her hand slid from her throat to her small breasts, massaged, pinched, a wave of intoxication bearing her along without her realizing that she'd gone beyond play-acting to enter a messy world where she was her own witness — someone who had stripped herself of dissimulation, ridiculing herself: 'Orré Kaya, don't you have even an iota of shame? Tall as a maypole, you're still behaving like a crazy child!' And Kaya turned away from Chandika Ma to heed the witness. Her eyes flew open. She scrambled into her clothes, casting about her in utter despair. *Whatever happened? Where am I?* Shivering in the pale afternoon sun, she told herself she was all right, that nothing had happened to her, and nothing would.

As soon as Chhote reached the front of the temple, he looked for Kaya on the steps. She wasn't there, nor in the courtyard. He'd raced up the path, but still Kaya seemed to have beaten him to it.

A frustrated Chhote stared at the ragged pennants flapping in the wind around the temple. People from the surrounding hamlets put them up as tokens of wish-fulfilment — when installed these would be bright, but the sun, wind and snow bleached and tore them to tatters. Now the pennants only made gibbering noises.

Chhote headed into the empty courtyard. A brass bell hung in mid-air. When it resounded echoes rolled off the mountains, the hills shrieked, and Chhote looked from one to the other in wonder. It seemed to Chhote that he was sitting right at the top — above the town, the panting woods — far from home, with nothing between him and the vast sky. The silence in the courtyard set off by the soughing woods was frightening. In fear, Chhote lost sight of everything — including the fact that, even as he waited for Kaya on the quadrangular platform facing the shrine, she was somewhere inside.

Chhote heaved himself off the platform and ambled round the shrine. He had a problem: at his age he was condemned to tag along behind his elders but, at the threshold of their world, he would be turned away — truly a piteous condition, yet no one pitied him — Kaya least of all! Not that he himself ever felt the need for pity, not even when he trailed behind Kaya like her shadow. He might feel let down, and lonely, that Kaya should have sneaked away to Mangtu's while he was asleep, but he did not pity himself. Anything was possible in his world. Anything that came to pass he accepted as a matter of course. He didn't expect to have Kaya all to himself. He was content with the scraps of memories she left him to play with when she was away. He teased these scraps as a dog teases a bone for lost clues.

Chhote peered in and saw Kaya squatting like a statue before the idol. He found the courage to call to her: 'Kaya, O Kaya!' But that neither roused the pujari from his sleep nor make Kaya look around. The monkeys, though, bounded noisily across the wooden roof.

Then he heard the temple bell ring behind him and thought optimistically that someone else must have come up at last — people rang the bell at the entrance as though they needed to draw Kali Ma's attention before coming in.

He ran out into the courtyard, but no one was there. The bell was swinging, humming to itself, in the wind. Whispers rose from the wood to fall to pieces at the temple. Some fragments clung to the ceiling, some cradled the bell, yet others romped about the water-tap. Frightened by the deep silence, Chhote diverted himself with playing on the flagstones. As he hopped on one foot from one stone to another, he said to himself that this one was Meerut where Lama had her home, this was Delhi where Babu had gone, this the railway station of Summer Hill, where Chacha lived with his son Beeru and where Kaya would be going soon.

Where Kaya would soon be going. . . . It sounded dreadful. Chhote's foot lingered on the flagstone, as if it were alien. This was Summer Hill, where the train stopped for three minutes on its way from Delhi, when both Kaya and he would gaze at the thicket beyond the far end of the railway platform to fleetingly glimpse Chacha's villa as the train plunged into the tunnel ahead.

The fear of Kaya leaving before long stared at Chhote from its lair beneath the paving stones, like an animal which merges into the background by changing its colour. It was everywhere, yet nowhere. Chhote had never known death, but to him, young as he was, going away — absence, missing someone — was no less than death. It touched Chhote with its invisible finger, and he started: *What is it? Who is there?* Later, he remembered nothing — neither the nudge of the finger nor the malevolent eyes of the crouching fear. What stuck in his memory, though, was the desolate afternoon, the tearful resentment. Chhote stamped on the flagstone that was the Summer Hill station, and yelled: 'Kaya, O Kaya! You wretch!'

Kaya shut her eyes tight. Chhote's yell burst into flashes of red that scattered among the red paste-marks on Kali Ma's blue-black body, weaving across her thoughtful countenance before she smilingly gathered them together on her garland of demons' skulls. Kaya's impulse was to sink her nails into Chhote's insolent face, but she pulled herself together and let her damp fingers unclench. The coral string lay coiled tight in her sticky palm.

Kaya recalled Dai Ma's words. Mother's strange sickness, her gasps for breath, the ill-formed chunk of raw flesh between her parted legs — each of these seemed to stick to the coral beads. Kaya was going to leave all of this behind at the holy feet of Kali Ma, certain that the goddess would assimilate them in her divine being to dispel the terrors of this long winter. No one would ever get to know about this afternoon . . . Kaya opened her eyes as something plopped to the floor.

She gazed at her palm, now empty — and shaking, not from cold or fear but like a snow-laden branch when the snow falls off it. She looked about nervously. Kali Ma, anointed with vermilion, stood still amidst wilted flowers and sugar puffs, watching her with a curious, cautious expression. The serpent-like coral string, clammy with moisture from Kaya's palm, lay coiled and glistening at the feet of the Goddess.

Kaya stared at her empty hand. A whiff of stale air reeled crazily up from her fingers. 'Kaya, *Orré* Kaya! You wretched girl!'

Chhote's yell subsided, as though soaked up by the temple walls. Kaya was no longer sure if it was Chhote who had called to her. It seemed like no ordinary call, a secret beckoning, assertive, soothing and reassuring, the kind that she'd wait for on the gallery of her home: a yearning, it throbbed in her blood. *I'll not want to lose it*, Kaya told herself. *If ever Lama returns she'll be surprised. She might not say a word, but she'll certainly think I've changed. In the pale daylight inside the temple Kaya suddenly felt she was another person crawling out of her former self, unknown to others — as when she once lay naked on the gallery in the dead of night listening to the call of her double, much like an animal which, without a conscious mind, senses anew in the silence of whispering bushes something turn on its side within it — which can recognize that silence, whispers, the turning within, belong really in the alien world of illusions, the lure of illusions, the tyranny of temptation.* Kaya could not carry this thought further. She tried to take a step forward but felt giddy; her breath faltered. She put up the red flag of danger at that point and retreated.

She started down to where Chhote was waiting for her on the steps.

By the time Kaya came out of the temple the sun had waned

and lengthening shadows sprawled close together over the steps. Chhote sat there alone, withdrawn, piqued. Kaya slouched down next to him. For a while they listened quietly to the breeze over their heads.

'Did I take too long?' She brushed her fingers through his hair.

Chhote said nothing, but his anger was already beginning to drain away.

'What have you been up to?' Chhote looked askance at her.

'I was trying to listen.'

'Didn't you hear me?'

You must be crazy. Must you yell like that?

Chhote flung her hand off his head. He felt like walking away, leaving her abandoned; but then he glimpsed his own yawning loneliness and changed his mind.

'I was playing by myself', he said slowly.

'Oh!' Kaya looked away at the hills.

'Each flag was a city, Kaya.'

'I heard you playing', she said. For a moment she was tempted to confide in him about the string of corals, of how her hand had suddenly emptied, of the curious look that Kali Ma seemed to give her — but she held her tongue, for that must remain a secret between her and Kali Ma, ever to be kept from anyone else's gaze.

Silence spun out between the two. The breeze ruffled the forest as it would the surface of a calm pond. The branches of trees swung apart, releasing birds that rose careening into the air.

'Shouldn't we go?' Chhote shivered in the cold.

'Yes, we should', said Kaya, without budging.

The bell rang in the temple behind them.

'Chhote, will you do me a favour?'

'What's it?'

'You'll take care of my things when I'm gone to Chachaji's, won't you?'

'I took care of your things last year too.'

Kaya leaned her head on his shoulder.

'When will you be back, Kaya?'

'I'll be gone about a month — till Babu comes back from Delhi', said Kaya slowly, lest her hopes spill over. Babu's coming was always an event to look forward to. A month at Chachaji's would, she suspected, stretch out like a desert — but the memories of her things at home, which had stood solidly by her so far, would again stand her in good stead: she could rely on her memories to see her through a desert any time.

'So will you take care of my things?'

'Well, what happens if Lama comes and asks for any of them?'

Kaya looked up. The late afternoon winter sun lay in tatters over the hill town.

'She won't come here again — she won't', she mumbled in a voice so low that Chhote could barely hear her. He was upset, for in entrusting her things to him she seemed to be preparing to go away for good. Kaya could earmark time into portions of days and months, and so console herself. But not Chhote. Time for him was indivisible, infinite, endless; to him every event partook of eternity, so that whoever left seemed to be going away for all time. A storm broke within Chhote. Kaya turned his face towards herself. His large eyes shone with unshed tears.

'Look, I'll be back before long — you won't even notice my absence.' She hesitated, weighing the deepening gloom around her with the gloom in Chhote's eyes. 'You won't notice it at all!'

'Will Chacha let you come away?' Chhote looked squarely at Kaya.

'Why not?' Kaya flared up. 'He can't stop Babu, can he?'

Chhote was easily convinced: indeed, nobody could stop Babu. On his way back from Delhi, Babu would get down at Chachaji's to pick up Kaya. Chhote recalled how in years gone by he'd watch him come down the hill with Kaya in front holding his walking-stick. It was a memory, a milestone that would sustain him through the long month. The house really opened up after Babu's arrival, and Mangtu started keeping a glowing brazier in his room too.

'It'll snow after you leave', observed Chhote.

Kaya laughed. 'How do you know?'

It snowed last year too, Chhote remembered. He remembered waking up in the middle of the night to find Kaya's bed empty and a stretch of white outside the window. An association between the two, the empty bed and the snowfall, came to hold his imagination, but he did not mention it to Kaya.

'Chhote', Kaya mumbled in a distant, deadpan voice.

'Did you say something?' Chhote was suddenly frightened by her tone.

'Forget it.'

'Come on now!'

'Do you ever think of Lama?' asked Kaya dredging the bottom of an inner silence.

Chhote kept quiet, as though Kaya had posed him a difficult question. In the fading light he could almost see Lama over his shoulder, awaiting his answer with bated breath.

'I do,' he said, 'whenever I go out.'

'Where?'

'By the railway station . . . down there I feel she's still some-where around, somewhere close by.'

'You mean the railway line — across that, don't you?'

She was staring hard at Chhote.

Did Ginny really die?

Someone seemed to snigger close behind them in the dusky light. They shuddered involuntarily, wondering for a moment if there really was somebody else with them, but it was an illusion — not uncommon in the mountains where light and shadow play constantly. They were just by themselves.

Was Ginny really dead?

Kaya had known about death but no proof of it — none of living, none of dying. She had never dared to extract from Lama, who had been in the thick of it, any reassurance, even a fistful of trust. Lama had washed her hands of it all, turned her back on the cold walls, gone her way.

I wish that I too could get away, thought Kaya.

This thought, no more than a flicker, nevertheless confounded and frightened her. At once she let the hidden, the inward, door click shut, and drew Chhote close to herself.

They both sat quietly in the darkness and on the steps of the temple for some time.

'There! Did you hear someone laugh, Kaya?'

'There's no one else here. Just us.'

They started down the stone steps.

Seven

They were steadily progressing up the hill.

The Kali temple was now far behind. They were on to the last incline. Neither spoke. Kaya's eyes watered, her nose ran. Bua's breath plumed in the cold.

They halted for breath on reaching the Ridge.

No more slopes ahead. The ground opened out here. The Mall meandered below, Jakhu Peak rose above. A pale November sun shone on the cold, green benches along the Ridge. The entire town lay shivering in the winter chill.

They were high above the town.

The sky was spotted with fluffy clouds that gathered by mid-day and concealed the snow-clad peaks. These drifted up the valley, apparently following the same route the two had taken. The houses on the hillside seemed to heave with the clouds.

They had walked halfway along the Ridge.

A tired Bua lowered herself on a bench. In summer a band played here and people sat on the benches to hear red-uniformed musicians led by their conductor who made florid gestures. The benches now lay vacant, there were no crowds around. Only the coolies and the rickshaw-pullers warmed themselves by a log fire. Blue smoke wreathed upwards into the clear air.

Bua looked out over the town. Kaya's eyes lingered on the church opposite and the road to Jakhu that skirted it. The Hardinge Library stood to her left. The sun glowed in the glass panes of its upper storey.

'Should we move, Bua?'

'Just a minute. We're almost there — what's the hurry?' Bua turned Kaya's face towards her.

'Do you see those roads we came up by?' Bua's excitement touched Kaya too. She let her eyes sweep down into the valley. The town took on a different look from here. The trees sprinkling the open spaces among the villas had transformed the whole into a lush wood, through which the squirrel roads went hopping down, carrying rooftops on their backs.

'See, that's the octroi-post', Bua exulted, as if she had solved a puzzle. 'Behind that hill is the Annandale ground, though we can't see it from here. And down there is your Babu's house.'

Kaya gazed past Bua's pointing finger: the gallery at the back, Mangtu's quarters below, and between the two the black specks of Mrs Joshua trees; and the trellis around the house over which Mangtu looped the washing to dry, which beat in the wind all night.

And, above all, a gleaming blur of red — a magical glow — suspended in the dying sun above the gathering shadows.

Part Two

Above The Town

One

The gate stood wide open, its separate halves buried in bushes on the sides. Clearly, the gate hadn't been shut for ages.

There was a slope beyond the gate, and an oak there cast its dense shadow across the gravel path. A board was fastened to the trunk of the tree, on which was painted 'Falkland'. The sign was partly hidden so that only 'land', pointing towards the house, peeped through the pale, brittle leaves.

Not only was the ground riddled with potholes and boulders but it dipped erratically. Sometimes it seemed to fall off to the fields below, at other times to run right into the housetops above. The gravel path, though, followed faithfully its straight course to Falkland, where finally it came to rest.

Trees on either side intertwined into a dark thatch over the path. It was dark underneath even during the day. Crickets echoed insistently in the shadows. One could reach the house if one followed their sound.

There was light at the end of the path, and a blazing sky beyond. The house stood there like a leaping flame.

Chacha was on the veranda of his house. Was he expecting them — or was he just lounging? Kaya had been walking ahead of Bua all along, but on seeing Chacha, Bua overtook her and bounded up the steps to cling to him, letting the bundle in her hand drop to the floor.

She was crying.

His hand on her head, Chacha stared into space wordlessly.

Neither paid any attention to Kaya who stood below the steps, looking on impassively. She found it strange that Bua was weeping.

The woman who conducted herself like Napoleon among the rickshaw-pullers seemed to have shrunk beside Chacha.

At last Chacha's eyes fell on Kaya, and she went up the steps. Bua had grown calm in his arms.

He held off Bua gently.

'Did you come on foot?'

'We had to. Do you think it's easy to find a rickshaw?' Bua looked a little embarrassed. Tears still glistened in her eyes, on her nose-tip, and along the wrinkles in her face.

Chacha knitted his brow.

'You really are the limit! You should have at least thought of this poor girl.'

Kaya wanted to come to Bua's rescue and tell Chacha that she wasn't tired. But he had meanwhile picked up Bua's bundle and moved away. He turned round at the door.

'Is everything all right at home?'

He was looking straight at Kaya, as if she, not Bua, was supposed to answer.

'Well, you know that . . .' Bua strove to find the right words for what had earlier caused tears in her eyes, but Chacha did not wait for her. He turned to lift the bar on the door. 'This is for the monkeys', he smiled at Kaya. 'The door-chain is not safe enough — they can unhook it.'

Kaya gazed at him. He was younger than Babu but looked bigger. Everything about him was large — his head, his hands, his feet — though he was not ungainly. He walked on light feet. He opened the door with a slight push. Kaya could never believe such large hands had so gentle a touch. He seemed to possess a will even stronger than his powerful body.

Bua followed Chacha into the house. As Kaya stepped in after her, she noticed the sign on the glass pane that she had seen the previous year: *Attention please, steps ahead!* Two steps led down into the sitting room. Last year she had had to stand on her toes to see her reflection in the glass. Today she glimpsed it as soon as she entered, though she could not recognize herself at once: the two forlorn eyes of a stranger stared back at her.

From somewhere far-off came mournful animal cries, one dying yelp giving way to another.

'Those are jackals', Chacha cut in. 'They howl when darkness falls.'

Chacha went upstairs to his room, Bua to another. Left to herself, Kaya did not know what to do. She pulled a chair close to the window.

The light had faded. The horizon had shrunk into a purplish-red streak over the hills. The setting sun cast a pale glow on the wall opposite the window where Kaya sat alone in the darkening room.

What was she doing, Kaya asked herself, in this barren house in a wood resounding with the howls of jackals? She felt trapped — as though she would never be able to leave here, get out, go away. . . . Will every day be like this? It occurred to her that Chhote must be alone in his room, Mother in her bed, Mrs Joshua's letter-box snapping open and shut again and again. There were no such familiar sounds here, nothing that could nudge her memories — except the dreary words on the door: *Attention please, steps ahead!*

Next to the drawing room was the library, and beyond it Beeru's room. Opposite, on the other side of the sitting room, stood the dining table. Tall, glass-fronted cabinets lined the walls. A flight of stairs took off from among these to Chacha's room. Kaya lingered at the foot of the stairs, intrigued that there should be a staircase inside the house rather than outside.

Chacha was upstairs — but she did not look up, having no intention of going to him. Instead, she made her way to the room on the far side of the library. The door was closed, but light escaped in a thin bar from under it to scatter on the floor of the library.

Kaya stood still in the dark, her ears picking up a sound . . . no, not just a sound but a stream of sounds, slow drawn-out notes — as if the stream, its languid flow arrested awhile, had run splashing on to a rock below — dazzling, winding through the unlit house.

She wanted to push open the door to see who was there, but could not overcome hesitation. Closed doors in unknown houses had always put her off. Even the houses deserted in winter in her neighbourhood seemed sinister. Both Chhote and she would avoid them.

She thought she had better go over to Bua, who would be waiting for her. Even as she turned, the door was opened. The bar of light at once leaped into her face to blind her.

Beeru appeared in the open door.

Kaya stood rooted to her spot. They stared at each other in silence.

Kaya could not bring herself to believe that the boy in the doorway was Beeru. Her memories of him fluttered about forlornly in the moment between doubt and recognition.

'When did you come?' Beeru threw the door wide open.

'In the evening.'

'Papa had told me you would.' He fixed his gaze on her. 'Did Mangtu come with you?'

'No. I came with Bua.'

'Lama's mother?'

Kaya nodded.

'Would you like to come in? There's still time for dinner.'

Beeru turned, and the light fell on half his face — longish, delicate, thick eyelash shadows under his eyes. Tall as Chacha, the hands by his sides as large as Chacha's. . . . His appearance convinced Kaya that the boy she had known as Beeru last year was now certainly someone else.

Kaya followed Beeru, forgetting all about Bua. Her eyes fell on the fireplace and the half-burnt twigs in it. A bed lay with its headrest against the wall. In front of the bed squatted an easy-chair. A piano stood below the window.

'Were you playing on *that*?' Kaya looked at the keys of the piano, surprised that the dazzling notes she had just heard should have emerged from such a bulky thing: she had never seen a piano before.

'Papa bought it from an Englishman who wanted to dispose of his things, including books, before leaving.' Beeru sat on his bed.

'An English woman lives on the ground floor of our house, too', said Kaya, even as it struck her that Mrs Joshua had nothing which she could leave behind — except a gramophone and some records.

Silence fell between the two. Beeru glanced at her a little uncertainly.

'Babu's away in Delhi, isn't he?'

'Yes', said Kaya, nodding.

'Your mother had a stillbirth?'

Kaya simply stared at him.

'Didn't you see it?'

'What?'

'The baby.'

'No', Kaya lied — but perhaps it was not a deliberate lie, for Kaya had never thought of that slimy lump in Dai Ma's hands as a baby. A baby had hands and feet, on which it crawled. Kaya had never tried to put into words what she had seen from the window in her home that night. What Beeru said did not seem to relate to her world of fragmented, formless memories. The superior airs that she assumed with Chhote forsook her.

'What's the matter?'

Kaya started, a smile on her lips. 'Nothing', she said.

'How you've grown, Kaya!'

'Well!' Kaya felt she was disclosing a secret: 'When I came in today, I could see my full face in the glass pane at the entrance.'

'And earlier you'd see only half of it?'

'No, I couldn't see it at all.' Kaya was glad she could talk with Beeru in a manner that was impossible with Chhote — or even with Lama, who wouldn't bother to listen to her carefully.

Kaya saw a pair of knitting needles and a ball of white wool on the bed.

'What's that?'

'It's an unfinished sock.'

'You knit?' asked Kaya, surprised.

'Yes, I do.'

'Being a boy?'

'What has knitting got to do with being a boy or girl?' Beeru caressed the wool contentedly.

The sight of Beeru's downy, fair taper-fingers somehow made Kaya feel ill at ease.

'What about you? Can *you* knit?'

Kaya shook her head.

'I enjoy it', continued Beeru. 'Don't you think it's fun knitting socks, gloves, little sweaters?'

'What do you do with them?'

'I undo them.'

Kaya looked up at Beeru's placid face. It struck her that with his piano, the clean tidy bed, the ball of knitting wool, he was far from her own wild, unpampered world of darkness.

'You live here alone?'

'Alone? What do you mean?'

'No one seems to enter your room.'

'Well, the pahari does. Papa drops in at night. Then there's the music teacher who comes twice a week.'

'Who is the pahari?'

'He works for us — you haven't been to the kitchen?'

Kaya saw for the first time a certain tightening in Beeru's pale face, the shadow of an inner conflict that, even as it passed, seemed to leave a mark behind, unlike in other people.

Someone knocked at the door, but didn't open it. Startled, Kaya looked at the closed door.

'They've sent for you. Dinner must be ready.'

'You won't eat?'

'I eat early.' Beeru's tone had changed. He sounded indifferent and aloof, and slightly sad.

Kaya stood up to leave. She turned about at the door — somehow it seemed odd leaving like this. Beeru had gone back to his knitting. 'I'll be back', she said.

Beeru lifted his head, a gentle smile on his lips. 'You'll find me here', he said, looking at Kaya until she left the room.

By the time Kaya reached the dining room, Bua and Chacha were already at the table, but waiting for her. Pulling up a chair, she stole a glance at Bua. Bua had washed up and changed into a fresh sari. Kaya had never seen her eating at a dining table before — at home she'd eat squatting on the floor. Perhaps Bua was also conscious of this, for she seemed to shrink into herself as she talked with Chacha over her food.

'Did you meet Beeru?' Chacha looked up from his plate.

'Yes', said Kaya swallowing a mouthful so hurriedly that it made her eyes water. Seen through her wet eyes, Bua and Chacha's faces seemed to be swimming.

'She loiters about the streets the whole day', said Bua. 'Now she can settle down to a few days of quiet.'

Perhaps Chacha didn't hear her: his gaze was riveted to something in the middle of the table.

'Who? Who loiters?'

'This girl, who else?' But Bua herself wandered off. The exertions of the long climb weighed in her bones. Sighing, she pushed her plate away.

'The house looks so deserted.'

'What do you mean?' Chacha peered at Bua, a little ruffled, perhaps offended. He had made his home here many years ago and by now had forgotten his earlier life. He had even forgotten that he once had a wife — Beeru's mother — who would potter about the house all day and at night spread her bed beside his. There are some people who leave no void, not even memories, when they die.

The house seemed perfectly agreeable to Chacha.

'Sometimes I think I should buy this house', Chacha said to Bua. 'If I have to live here, why not buy it? Why pay rent all my life?'

Bua started, as if suddenly woken up from sleep.

'You mean you intend to stay put here the rest of your life?' Bua always wondered why Chacha had wanted to stay on in these hills after retiring from the army. Babu had a job and a family to tend to, but Chacha could have lived comfortably anywhere else: he wasn't burdened with domestic problems — there was only Beeru, and he could have lived anywhere.

What bound Chacha to this place?

'Tell me, where else can I go?'

'Am I to tell you? Both you brothers keep away from me — every year I come running after you to this remote place two or three times just to look the two of you up. Have you ever given me a thought?'

Chacha turned pale, as though Bua had touched a raw nerve. 'I've asked you so often to stay with me, but you always turned that down, apparently because of Lama. What pretext do you have now? Are you afraid the mountains will devour you, or what?'

Bua sighed deeply, as though her life itself loomed ahead like another mountain. She had spent her years in the dust and grime of distant cities, she certainly wasn't worried by the hills or the illusions that they might engender.

'No, the mountains won't do anything to me. But they will devour both of you one day.'

Kaya expected Chacha to burst out laughing: how could the mountains ever devour anyone? They had neither teeth nor jaws nor the cruelty of man. She was thus surprised when Chacha remained quiet, a little hurt perhaps, as if Bua had put her finger on a spot where he felt least secure, where a danger — though not fear — lurked all the time.

Chacha looked at Bua with stricken eyes. 'Look, it should be possible for you to put up with our brother if not with me. He has a family. Besides, you like it there, too — don't you?'

'You call that a family?' Bua hissed contemptuously. 'He himself lives in Delhi while his children wander the hillside like orphans and the wife the empty rooms. Poor, lonely woman! I tell you it was a mistake to have ever sent Lama over — and now you want *me* to move in for good?'

Red in the face, Bua restrained herself because of Kaya.

Kaya, though, had meanwhile wandered off, her attention caught by the mist that was drifting in through the open doors, windows, ventilators. It would rain, she thought; it always did whenever the mist sailed into one's house. Lightning would flash across the dark library, the chairs, Beeru's closed door.

In all this a young pahari servant ran panting in and out to replace the empty vegetable bowls or the plate of chapattis before disappearing into the darkness again. It seemed to Kaya that she was seeing the boy through a mist of sleep — a Nepali with close-cropped hair, round-faced, his cheeks like apples coated with grime. Perhaps he was the pahari Beeru had told her about. The boy didn't even stop to catch his breath nor glance at anyone — not even at Kaya, a newcomer; he just tipped his plate of chapattis on to the plate before withdrawing hurriedly. Kaya listened to his receding footsteps on the stairs below. Sleepily, then, she waited for him to reappear like a gnome from another world, waxing and waning by turns. Kaya was unaware that Bua and Chacha had stopped talking. The rain pattered on the window-panes. Kaya dreamed that she was watching the pahari from her own window, that he was carrying a heapful of chapattis, that the chapattis were getting soaked in rain . . .

'She's gone to sleep', Kaya heard Chacha say as he stood over her. He reached out to shake her.

It was raining outside. Bua gathered used plates and placed them at a corner of the table. Chacha stood about idly, as if undecided about something. He patted Kaya on the head and turned away. 'I'm going out for a while — don't wait up for me', he said to Bua. He took his umbrella. 'Go to sleep, you're tired.' Then he went down the stairs.

Out in this rain?

But Bua didn't ask him why. She took Kaya's hand to help her off the chair, and led her to the spare room they were to share.

Kaya was wide awake by now. They crossed the library on their way to the guest room. Kaya's eyes strayed to Beeru's door. It was closed. No sounds from inside: he must have gone to sleep. She stagge ed along behind Bua who almost dragged her.

As they went into their room Kaya's feet fell upon a soft rug. For a moment she thought she was back in Mrs Joshua's flat. The same florid wallpaper, the same stale odour. It seemed the room had not been aired for ages.

There were two beds in the room with a jug of water and two glasses on a tripod between them. Old tin trunks had been pushed under the beds where mice could occasionally be heard scampering. Except for cobwebs in the corners, the walls were bare. It seemed that the room had not been used for a very long time.

Bua stood still for a while. 'Whenever I come here, I can't help thinking of your Chachi', she said turning to Kaya.

'Was this her room?'

'Yes, this was her room. You might not remember anything about her — you were too young then.'

Bua undid her bundle of clothes to separate Kaya's. The tin roof above screamed under the beating rain. How different the rain sounds in somebody else's house!

Bua looked intently at Kaya, stepped over to the side of her bed, and rested her hand on Kaya's shoulder.

'What comes over you, Kaya?'

'Why, what's happened?' Kaya glanced up, suddenly afraid.

'You keep staring into emptiness.' Bua's voice grew soft and gentle. 'I've been seeing you for some days. You often have such a faraway look in your eyes.' She seemed to delve deep within her. 'You wander away every now and then — are you all right?'

Kaya moved aside. Bua's hand slid off her shoulder.

Kaya laughed.

'Why, Bua, I'm right here — in front of you.'

Bua drew in a long breath and turned back as if despairing both of the girl and the world at large.

Kaya lay on her bed. She listened to the patter of the rain on the roof. She could see nothing beyond the clouds through the window — just a dull grey sheet that lightning periodically ran through, sharp as a knife.

'Did you hear?'

'Yes, Bua?'

'Someone's coming up the stairs.'

At first Kaya heard nothing, then the house seemed to shake. She sat up, looking towards the door she saw a shimmering spot of light in the sitting room: there was someone there with a torch.

'Lie down', Bua said calmly. 'It must be Chacha.'

'Was he out all this time?'

Bua did not answer. Kaya listened to her breathing settle into an even rhythm: Bua had had a fright but now she was all right.

There seemed nothing to worry about now, torchlight or no torchlight; the house had steadied. Kaya lay down again. She was cold in her bed. Had she been in her own room at home, she'd have asked Chhote over and warmed her shivering legs against his. She missed him dreadfully. One realizes how vile, how wicked, absence can be only when one is entirely on one's own. Then it struck her that Bua too would be leaving in the morning. A knot formed in her belly at the thought. It slithered up to her throat like a gecko on a cold wall, and she hugged herself tightly.

'Are you cold?' enquired Bua.

Kaya feigned sleep but that did not stop her from shivering.

Bua heard her shiver: darkness gives away every little groan. She rose to tuck her extra blanket about Kaya, then sat on the edge of her bed.

'You won't be lonely here, Kaya — will you?'

Kaya kept quiet.

'I'd have stayed but your mother is alone. She wouldn't even let me come here.'

She could let me go, though, thought Kaya bitterly. Anger welled inside her. She was angry with her mother and even more so with the mysterious things happening around her. But she could not talk of these to Bua, who was herself engulfed by problems she did not say a word about.

Bua supposed Kaya had gone to sleep and so went back to her own bed. 'How long will it continue to rain?' she muttered under her breath. 'How can I get to sleep with this ratatat on the roof?' She rolled over on her side in the darkness, her face towards Kaya.

Kaya too was awake, her eyes shut. Where had Chacha been so late? She was reminded of the Nepali boy who served them chapattis. The kitchen must be downstairs, she thought. That boy must have a small room, like Mangtu's. All servants lived in identical rooms, dark and dingy, full of bidi smoke but warm. . . . It seemed to Kaya when she closed her eyes that she had entered another darkness, different from the darkness in this room; there she was free, on her own, in her own house she could escape across time and space and reach out to Chhote and see Babu stoop over her in bed: she was her own mistress there, she could cry without shame, find solace in tears, let go . . .

So many things flood one's mind before sleep takes over!

Two

Bua couldn't leave the next day. Not only did Chacha insist that she stay, but it also rained. The rain fell continually for two days.

The clouds cleared on the third day. Chacha sent for a rickshaw despite Bua's objections. Bua was embarrassed about the rickshaw. Wordlessly, she thrust her bundle on to the seat before climbing in, her back to us. Chacha was accompanying her up to the Mall. No sooner had the rickshaw started than it stopped. Kaya thought Bua might have something to say to her. She burst into a run, but Bua had apparently changed her mind, for the rickshaw pulled out before Kaya could reach it. She ran another few steps, then pulled up under the oak which bore the Falkland sign, wet from the rain.

The rickshaw disappeared down the main road but the sound of its bell still floated up.

Bua had gone, yet Kaya could not bring herself to believe that she would not find her in the house when she got back to it, that Bua's bed piled with her clothes would be empty beside hers.

She turned back along the path. Sharp pointed stones, washed by the rain, stuck out through the slush. The trees shrugged off raindrops clinging to their branches. Kaya calmed herself with the thought that Bua's leaving was just another pothole in the way that she wouldn't even look back on later. She had already learnt to put up with so much. Babu's rickshaw used to disappear likewise. From the veranda she would watch it grow into a blur as it crawled away like a worm up the steep slope, and, to her surprise, she would discover that her pain too blurred with the rickshaw's disappearance. Nothing more to it afterwards — unless one deliberately went about scratching the scab or kept on turning round for yet another look into the pothole . . . Kaya would rather not dwell on it; she'd let it be.

This too was a kind of happiness, even if lacking in reassurance. Those were happy days, though Kaya did not realize that — for happiness can only be recognized in retrospect, only when the pangs of childhood are forgotten. At the time, Kaya was unaware of the moments when she leaped clear of pain and into happiness, or when happiness suddenly turned into pain. Such things were still beyond her.

In those days there was much that was beyond her.

The previous night's rain had narrowed the pathway, the red soil of the hillside having washed over it. It was slippery underfoot. Beeru stopped from time to time to check that Kaya was still behind him.

'Beeru!'

'I'm here.' His face showed up among the trees.

It was the sort of clear day that is typical in the mountains after the rain, with the fields in the valley, still flooded, looking like small lakes.

Beeru had appeared in Kaya's doorway earlier in the afternoon. He looked around the room, his quiet gaze lingering on her bed, her nightdress on the bed, the books she'd brought with her, the ribbons and hairpins on the night-table.

'Want to come along for a walk?'

'Where?'

'There are several spots near by.' Beeru raised his long, thick eyelashes. 'You hardly ever step out.'

'I don't know where to go.'

'There's an old church here built by the English.'

'Is it far off? Should I change my clothes?'

Beeru observed her kameez let out at the hem, her toes poking out from her chappals, her eyes keen and hungry in her tousle-headed, pale face.

'You'd better put on a jacket or something — it'll be cold up there.'

As they made their way up they carefully avoided the slippery mud and ditches. The path wove through terraced fields. They had left the tarred road far behind. Once in a while they would hear the buses and lorries plying far below. They peered through the trees to see the toy-like traffic speeding away towards the town. The silence continued to hum long after the vehicles went out of sight.

'How far do we still have to go?'

'Are you tired?'

Beeru was amazed that anyone could get tired so soon. He himself would walk for hours on end and had followed this very path right up to Jakhu Peak many times.

The path clung to the hillside, well above the motor road but below Jakhu. A yellow blur crept along overhead. It was the sun, looking in the November mist like a fuzzy electric bulb suspended from a blue ceiling.

Sometimes Kaya would forget Beeru as they walked up the winding path — until he emerged again round the next bend. He was wearing a full-sleeved turtle-necked pullover, his hair fell low over his forehead, he had slanting, narrow eyes in a broad face, like the Japanese, and, above all, he had long thick eyelashes, so thick that someone behind him could see them if his face turned sideways. When he stopped to ask her if she was tired, his concern flustered Kaya, for it brought to mind the nights when Babu knocked at her door before coming in with that curious, at once anxious and tender, expression that was now reflected in Beeru's calm, steady eyes. In such moments a soothing, almost grain-textured gust would sweep through her, bringing a serenity that stilled the earlier tremulousness, like a breeze briefly stirring blossoms and soon leaving them tranquil, as though it had never been . . .

Suddenly they came upon an open stretch of level ground where Kaya found herself staring at an old wooden building, its facade black with age. Above the level ground a brick platform jutted out like the proscenium of a stage; the wooden building on it was a church.

A single row of flowering trees, their scarlet and velvety-blue flowers nameless but proud for having withstood the cold November rain, ran all around the ground. Some petals lay crushed in the mud under the trees.

Kaya had never seen such a profusion of flowers at this height.

Four wooden steps led to the platform. As Kaya went up, she saw Beeru in the half-open door of the church, leaning against the panel still in place; the other panel lay like a mutilated bird's wing in the dust among stones and grass.

'Is this the church?' Kaya asked without much enthusiasm.

'Well, what did you expect?' Beeru was a little surprised by her reaction.

'Nothing, really.'

She didn't tell him she'd been looking forward to seeing four lofty white spires, a belfry up in the front, and tall stained-glass windows — not this building gone to rack and ruin, a wretched skeleton of a church.

They went inside. The bare walls, the exposed roof of timber, seemed to enclose an emptiness. The place where the altar must have once stood had sunk beneath the splintered floorboards. A black cat crouched there. On seeing Kaya it leaped up and bolted through the open door.

'Well, this is all — there's nothing more beyond this.' Beeru already regretted bringing Kaya along.

Unmindful of Beeru, Kaya turned, moved to the right of the altar. The floor was uneven with most of the planking already gone, ripped up by people — much as vultures tear at a dead animal until only the bones remain.

She picked her way among the remains, her hand on the wall for support.

Suddenly a flurry of wings churned the stale air and something clammy grazed Kaya's cheek. She opened her mouth to call out to Beeru but her parched lips made no sound. Feeling dizzy, she sat there on the planks.

'You all right?' Beeru looked at her nervously. He was standing in front of a window and the feeble sun fell on his face.

'Something struck the side of my face', she said, trying to seem unruffled.

'Must have been a bat. Don't worry — they're harmless.'

Kaya had heard about bats but never seen one till then.

'Do you come here often?'

'Only sometimes — but no one in the household knows about this. Perhaps they don't even know there's a church around here.'

He still stood by the window, gazing at the setting sun lighting the tops of trees — an utterly different world from the dark, damp interior of the church.

'Does no one come here any more?'

'Who will?' said Beeru, somewhat disheartened. 'The English came earlier — we used to watch them from the bushes.'

'What did you see?'

'We saw them arrive by rickshaw. The girls had parasols over their heads and . . .' he hesitated before continuing, 'nothing on their legs — bare, hairless and white as wax. Unlike ours.'

'They wear nylon stockings, that's why.'

'Really? How do you know?' Beeru looked at Kaya suspiciously.

'Mrs Joshua lives on the ground floor of our house. Her legs are white, too.'

The musty dark in the church and white legs — these apparently had no relation to each other, and so they fell silent.

A cobweb stirred in a gust. The glow outside lit another section of the broken stained-glass panes.

'Did you see this?' said Beeru, moving from the window towards a large niche.

Kaya then saw two old pieces of timber placed one across the other — and nailed to this, through the palms, the naked body of a man, head sunk on the chest. A spot of sun lay close to his feet, one foot over the other, also pierced. Large blood-splattered nail holes stared back at her from the two-piece frame eaten through by woodworm. She wanted to reach out a hand and run her fingers gently over those gaping wounds. But she held back as something unknown forbade her. She was surprised by this, for she had never before seen a 'No' sign loom up through the air, and that too in a tumbledown church where there was no one to stop her.

Kaya snapped out of her spell as a shadow passed over the

figure on the cross. She turned her head towards the door to check if somebody had come in. No one had.

Only Beeru stood there.

'Look,' she wanted to say to him, 'something just came in through that door — did you see it?' But the words died on her lips as she looked into Beeru's calm, aloof, unafraid eyes. All those things that had been troubling her not long ago — the bats, the stale air, the close space, the figure on the cross — instantly receded when she saw him. Could someone suddenly fill those inner spaces where unease and fears were lodged?

'We should go', said Beeru. As he moved away, sunlight spilled in over the split beams.

'So soon?' Kaya was disappointed. 'Can't we remain here a little longer?'

'They might worry about us at home. You will be staying here; we can come again another day.'

Kaya shook her head, once, twice, dejectedly.

'No, we can't — I won't be staying here long.'

Beeru looked slightly upset.

'How can you go — until Babu comes?'

'I'll run away.'

'You'll run away?' Beeru repeated her words, unable to say anything else.

Kaya herself was taken aback — she had spoken on a mere impulse; but now that those words were out she felt in the stillness of the church that she could do anything, say anything.

'Does that alarm you, Beeru?'

'What?'

'My running away', said Kaya with a self-deprecatory laugh, averting his eyes.

Beeru withdrew into himself: he visualized the safety of his room, his fireplace, his piano, his books — where there was peace, far from Kaya's restless unpredictability; he'd rather turn his back on her and retreat.

Kaya retreated, too, thinking of her part of the town, where there was a red tin roof — the only one of its kind, and a railway line lolling in the sun, and Mrs Joshua's letter-box that kept an eye on everything. It seemed impossible to her, this moment in the fading light near a church, that Beeru, standing in front of her, had no idea of any of these. The thought filled her with dread, as if her world was unreal, an illusion, or perhaps not even that, nothing at all. Only the church was real, and this boy, and this wounded man on the cross in the dark niche: this was the reality within which Bua had permanently left her.

Could she run away? No, she knew she had only been putting on an act, much like what she did on the gallery of her house when she shed her clothes — and she felt ashamed of herself. She knew she would not go away. She knew, too, that if only she could, she would lead Beeru by his hand to this truth, and tell him he need not worry, that she wasn't going away, she could cope, there was nothing in all this that she could not tackle.

She looked up to tell this to Beeru, to reassure him — but was shocked to see that he was nowhere around. A dull grey light spread over the grimy rafters. Wispy clouds drifted in through the broken windows. 'Beeru', she said. The sound echoed off the walls, off the jagged burnt slats at her feet. She ran out. Beeru was waiting for her among the rocks and trees on the slope below.

She started climbing down the slope.

Together, they set off in silence. The sky was overcast. Long, black shadows had gathered on the hills.

'Why did you come away?'

Beeru kept quiet, and concentrated on the path. The wind blew his hair over his eyes.

'Are you annoyed?' Kaya's voice had a faint tremor in it.

Beeru stopped, looking at her uncertainly. 'What were you thinking of in the church?'

'Nothing.'

'You were so silent that I thought you were praying.'

'What prayer!' she laughed. 'For whom?'

'You looked so absorbed as you stood there before . . .' Beeru broke off. What could he tell her about the figure on the worm-eaten cross?

'Who is he, Beeru?'

'Don't you know? They pray to him.'

'But who is he?'

'He was crucified. He died for everyone.'

Kaya gave him a quizzical look. 'For everyone?'

'I don't know — I only read about it in a book.'

Beeru said no more.

As Kaya walked down the path she told herself that she would return one of these days to the church and have a good look at the man on the cross in the dark niche, he who had died for everyone.

Three

Kaya awoke as the door opened hesitantly. Her eyes turned towards the door: who could it be at this hour?

There was no one there. The sound she thought she heard had been too faint anyway. Drowsy from a late siesta, for a moment she could not make out where she was. Her hand groped along the bed near hers: it was empty.

It was odd, thought Kaya, that her hand should still reach out to the other bed the moment she woke up, even though so many days had passed since she left home.

Someone knocked on the door.

Was it Beeru or Chacha?

But the face wrapped round the door belonged to neither.

'Will you eat now, or later?' It was the pahari, his gaze skimming the semi-dark room in search of her.

'Come in.'

'Were you sleeping?' The boy stared at Kaya, his enormous eyes widening in astonishment. He wore a shirt, buttonless — and an ochre, tasselled Balaclava cap that covered both his ears and chin.

'Isn't Sahib home yet?'

'He'll be late.'

'And Baba? Where is he?'

Baba, that's what the boy called Beeru.

'He's gone out with his music teacher.'

Kaya recalled that Beeru often saw his teacher home.

So neither Beeru nor Chacha was in.

She sat up hurriedly when she saw the boy turning to leave.

'Wait', she called out. She didn't normally mind being by herself for hours together. But as soon as it dawned on her that she was alone in this house she felt the walls lunge at her.

'What is it, Chhoti Bibi? Shall I turn on the light?'

'No, it's not dark enough yet.'

Outside, the last of the light still lingered on the hills. In her home it would get dark early, but Chacha's house was built on a height so that the light off the hilltop shone in the window-panes until much later.

'May I go, then?' The boy regarded her with his round, innocent eyes, shifting his weight from one leg to the other.

'Where will you go?'

'To my room.'

'Where is it?'

'Just behind the house, at the end of the path down there. Didn't you know?'

Kaya contemplated the boy silently.

'No, I haven't been there.'

'Want to come along?'

'May I?'

'Why not?'

Kaya was tempted, then had her doubts. There was something in it that seemed wrong, quite wrong, that she needed to talk over with Chacha beforehand. She tried to keep the thought of the empty house at bay. If only Beeru were around!

'Aren't you coming?' The boy looked at her uncertainly; he realized she could change her mind.

'Go ahead — I'll join you later.'

Kaya quickly slipped on her blue frock — the only one that she'd brought with her. It was her school dress, still smelling of the classroom. Both its oversize pockets, reaching down almost to her knees, still contained chalk and pencil butts. Her mother would insist on her changing into a salwar-kameez at home, but there was no one here to stop her.

The boy was waiting for her at the head of the stairs.

'Just a minute', the boy said to her. 'I'll bring a torch. It's dark down there.'

'There's no need to — I can do without one', Kaya insisted. She dreaded torchlight. She could put up with it in a room but not out in the open where it seemed to trace a dizzy zigzag in the dark. In any case, the light from the veranda was overflowing on to the slope below.

The crisp November leaves on the ground had been raked into heaps on the sides of the path. From a distance, these seemed to crouch in the darkness, as though ready to pounce on passers-by. A row of trees extended to the servants' quarters. These stood still unlike at home, thought Kaya: no fluttering of bird-wings, no rustling of leaves. But the stars overhead were as bright as those above her own gallery.

The boy stopped in his tracks.

In front were the two-storeyed quarters. The ground floor was engulfed in darkness. Light glowed in the two rooms on the upper floor.

'Come on!' Kaya gave the boy a nudge, but he stood stock-still.

'What's the matter?'

Suddenly, the boy then clasped Kaya's hand and started dragging her towards the pitch-dark shed behind the stairs.

Kaya, in a panic, let him do so.

He was panting, his breath hot near her.

There were footsteps above them.

Someone was coming down the stairs.

Kaya followed the boy's gaze.

'Who's there?'

'Keep quiet, Chhoti Bibi!'

An oblong of light from the rooms splayed over the steps.

It outlined Chacha.

Kaya stared at him: what was he doing here at this hour?

A big, burly man, he groped on the treads with his walking-stick.

He was soon on his way to the house. His shadow leaped up the trees as he walked away. Kaya could hear the dull thud of his cane long after he was gone.

'Let's go', said the boy stepping out from the shed, his face as calm as the calm night.

'Why did you have to hide us?'

The boy said nothing, but a secretive smile played on his lips. It struck Kaya that he was not as innocent as he looked. She had a similar opinion about Mangtu, too. These mountain people were all the same: they conducted themselves in an aura of frustrating mystery, distanced alike from innocence and guile.

Kaya had half a mind to turn back. Somehow, at the sight of Chacha her spirits had flagged, her ardour dampened. Her legs felt weak under her. If she could manage to, she would get away to her room — and fast.

'Don't you want to come up?'

The boy's voice was so earnest, so bright, that it seemed to Kaya she not only heard but saw it in the dark. It had an eagerness that could not be ignored.

It didn't take them long to reach upstairs. There was a narrow gallery enclosed by a trellis. It led to two rooms, one of which was the kitchen. The light in the kitchen was on, but there was nobody inside. A mat curtain hung over the door, opening into the other room. The room was lighted, yet it did not seem anyone was there either.

'Is no one inside?'

Kaya threw the boy a puzzled glance.

The boy raised the curtain and slipped in.

Kaya waited at the door.

Somewhere beyond the rooms stray dogs set up a chorus. Jackals howled too, not very far away.

The curtain lifted, and the boy reappeared, smiling broadly.

'Please come in.'

Kaya peered inside, expecting to see a room not unlike Mangtu's — with a burlap sack on the floor to sit on, a brazier to warm oneself by, ashes scattered all over, and a familiar acrid smell of tobacco smoke in the air.

But her gaze froze. A woman sat against the wall opposite, staring back at her with keen interest, hands folded on her lap, palms joined together — but failing to raise them in greeting. She was wearing a red petticoat. Her nose-ring sparkled white as a flower in the lamplight.

'Come in', said the woman, motioning Kaya to the mat in the middle of the floor.

Kaya looked round for the boy. He was sitting on the threshold, his legs stretched out in front of him, indifferent to both, apparently giving the howling jackals his undivided attention.

The jackals went on howling.

'Come on!' the woman urged, her voice thin but full-throated.

This time Kaya obeyed, and sat down crosslegged on the mat.

The room was very different from Mangtu's. A bed lay in a corner with a blue coverlet on it. The door that gave on to the kitchen bore glossies of film stars. A sewing machine covered in black stood on one side of the mat. A heavy box of galvanized sheet secured with a brass padlock took up the space behind the bed. Nothing about the room was even remotely reminiscent of Mangtu's. The thought occurred to Kaya that she had perhaps come to the wrong place, but she could not backtrack now. The woman, her nose-ring twinkling, was watching her closely.

Kaya pulled her frock over her folded legs. There was something in the woman's eyes that shamed her, and made her self-conscious.

'Has Badi Bibi gone back?' the woman asked gently.

'Who is Badi Bibi?' Kaya was wary.

'The one who came with you.'

'You mean, Bua? Did you see her?'

'The house is within sight of the quarters.' She laughed softly, her nose-ring quivering. She bore a strong resemblance to the boy. But her forehead was broader and her skin tinted a deeper yellow, so unnaturally yellow that it seemed the pigment would run if washed.

Kaya was drawn to the woman in spite of herself.

'You'll be staying here for some days, won't you?'

'Until December. Babu will come then.'

The woman nodded knowingly.

'Are you staying in the former Bibiji's room?'

'Did you know her?'

'In a way — I never saw her, though', she said, her voice low.

'Haven't you ever been to the house?'

'No, I don't go there.'

Kaya stared at her in disbelief. Only a short path separated the house from the quarters, and she could not imagine that those few yards would be so impossible a distance to negotiate.

The woman broke into a smile so broad and ingenuous that it seemed to transform her into a young girl again.

'I haven't been to the house but I know all that goes on in it. You know the room you're occupying is your father's favourite? He stays there on all his visits. But I don't remember ever seeing your mother — she's never been.'

'Have you met Babu?'

'How can I? I keep indoors.'

'Whenever he comes, he comes by rickshaw', the boy chipped in from where he squatted on the threshold.

Kaya had forgotten all about him.

'That's my son there.'

The boy grinned. Kaya found it strange that she should be sitting around here at all, in a room surrounded by darkness and howling jackals and clumps of trees, opposite a woman, a total stranger, who nevertheless knew everything about her. She was startled to think that, had she not taken the boy at his word, she'd have probably never met her, never even suspected that such a woman was living under their very noses.

The woman's nose-ring gleamed over her gleaming teeth. Her speech was full-throated, sharp and clear, yet timid. Her hands were concealed under her dupatta. Her feet, barely visible beneath the spread of her petticoat, were dyed with henna and she wore silver anklets, which reminded Kaya of Mangtu.

'You stay in here all day?'

'Where else!' The woman looked amused.

'Don't you ever go out?'

The woman shook her head, as if it was a foolish question. How could she put across to Kaya, still a child, that a woman's kitchen, the four walls of her house, made up her whole world?

'I once went down to see the waterfall', she conceded with a chuckle. 'Have you been to it yet?'

'I didn't know there was a waterfall here.'

'Why, didn't Chacha tell you?'

Kaya thought this question stood out from all the others, for her voice dropped when she said Chacha. Kaya saw a shadow cloud the woman's sallow face.

'You'd better go now. He must be waiting for you.'

It was not a command, but Kaya got up. For a while she couldn't make out who could be waiting for her. She could have sat here till all hours of the night.

'May I come again?'

'You want to?' The woman was surprised. 'But no one comes here.'

The boy gave his mother a quick glance, like a child who, when he catches his elders lying, would rather question his own understanding than mistrust them. Nevertheless, this is the child's first acquaintance with pain and, more than that, with the sense of shame.

He looked away, out into the darkness beyond the door.

The woman rose and came over to Kaya. 'Don't tell anyone you came here', she said before moving hurriedly towards the kitchen.

The boy went on gazing into the darkness, whistling absently between his teeth.

They stopped in front of the house.

'I must go back, Chhoti Bibi', the boy said. 'Can you go by yourself now?'

'Won't you come in?'

'I've got to prepare the dinner.'

'All right, I'll find my way back myself.'

Kaya saw the boy's shadow scurry through the trees to the servants' quarters.

She stood near the steps leading to the house, then jerked with surprise: all the lights in the house had been switched on.

Seeing the lit house, Kaya recalled a picture she had seen in an old book — of a ship anchored in darkness. In the clear November night the house looked like that ship. The long veranda with folding chairs set out on it was a deck. In the summer Chacha played cards here with his friends and treated them to food and drink, but they left for the plains by September. With their departure, the veranda started looking deserted. The empty chairs, the card table, the flowerpots: the ruins of a lost summer. Chacha now sat among these alone, nursing his drink, looking at the Sanjauli lights glimmering between two hills.

The view from the veranda was its main attraction. Jakhu Peak reared above to the right, the Sanjauli township shimmered in front, and Elysium-Round Hill on the left ran down to the residential area of Kaithu at the base, the undulating slopes bare at places, clad with the thick growth of trees at others. The houses lay haphazardly scattered all around, like a hastily dropped pack of cards. When the lights came on in the houses at nightfall, it seemed that fireflies had invaded the hillsides. Soon, mist would drift down to the valley, turning it into a lake of swirling white, in which floated hills, houses, fireflies; then the mist would lift and all these would re-emerge, bolder and brighter . . . so long as this play of mist and light lasted Chacha watched it quietly, sipping from his glass.

Chacha was sitting on the deck tonight, too.

'Who's there?' His voice echoed in the veranda.

Kaya had no time, nor the will, to retreat. She walked straight towards him.

'Ah, it's you!' As he raised his head, the lamp lit his face. 'Had you gone out?'

'Yes', Kaya nodded even as she saw in her mind's eye a dark figure descending the stairs outside the servants' quarters, wondering if it had really been Chacha or just her imagination that peopled the shadows at night.

'Were you out alone?'

'The pahari was with me', she said, aware that she was being only half truthful.

Chacha raised his glass for another sip.

'You like it here?'

'Yes, I do.'

'You don't miss your home any more?'

Kaya watched him warily. She wanted to reassure him she didn't miss anything any more, but that would have been another lie. She let it die in her dry throat.

'Your Babu doesn't feel at home here — he's always in a hurry to leave', said Chacha softly, with a slight laugh. Babu was his elder brother but he spoke of him so gently that it seemed he was younger. Chacha had been away in the army for so long that he had almost become an outsider to the family; perhaps to make up for that, he had become excessively attached to both Babu and Bua.

'Do you remember the first time you came here?'

'When was it?' Kaya was interested.

'You were only two years old then! Babu brought you along on a pony. Your Chachi was alive at the time. It was she who gave you your name, since you were a mere bag of bones.'

No, Chacha was not in his cups. He had always treated her like a grown-up, 'a jimmewar girl' in Mrs Joshua's words . . . and suddenly she felt she was on the verge of tears, a cloud churning inside her as memories of home flooded back.

'Mrs Joshua asked to be remembered to you.'

Chacha looked up from his glass. 'Don't tell me she's still alive!' He smiled, releasing web-like wrinkles which had thus far been concealed under his eyes. 'Some people live for ever, don't they?' he added.

Mist drifting over the valley obscured the stars to dull beads, somewhat like those sewn to the other side of the curtain on the door.

'You aren't cold, Kaya — are you?'

Kaya shook her head vigorously, dreading the thought of being sent inside. She was relieved to see that Chacha made no effort to get up either.

'Beeru isn't back yet?'

'He'll take some time — his teacher lives in Sanjauli.' Chacha looked at Kaya as another thought struck him. 'Did you see Beeru's piano?'

'Yes.'

'Did you know I got it free?' he said cheerfully. He talked with Kaya as he would with friends who called on him in summer. 'It came from Calcutta.'

'You went all the way to Calcutta to bring it?'

'I didn't — my letter did that!' His eyes lit up. 'I had nothing much to do in those days, so I busied myself with collecting things. I saw an ad in the *Statesman*. A Mr Wood wanted to dispose of his library, with the piano thrown in. He was leaving for England soon. He'd already sold all his other things. He wanted to give the piano only to the man who would buy all his books — and to none other.'

Chacha laughed happily, and took another swig from his glass.

'The piano was brand new,' he went on, 'but the books were brittle with age. Their pages started falling off in transit, like leaves in autumn!'

He fell silent, his hand flitting over the bottle, the water jug, his glass, like a stubborn moth, underscoring the quiet of the veranda.

Perhaps it was the mist or the weariness of a long day, but Kaya wanted to be near Chacha. She didn't quite know how to go about it. Still, she took the first faltering step: 'You went to the servants' quarters, Chacha?'

He did not move or raise his voice. 'You saw me?' he asked matter-of-factly.

'When you were coming down the stairs.'

His looked at Kaya quietly. This time he didn't lift his glass. 'Did you meet *her*?'

'Yes.' Kaya realized he wanted the truth, and felt suddenly light.

'You've grown up, Kaya — haven't you?' Chacha walked over to the railing. Nothing was visible any more through the pall of white over the hills. The trees, the house lights — all had been curtained off.

There were footsteps on the stairs and soon Beeru appeared. He seemed surprised to see Chacha and Kaya on the veranda, but he walked past them to his room without a word to either.

Chacha did not even glance at him.

Kaya went to her room immediately after dinner. She thought she would be able to fall asleep as soon as she lay down. The lights went out in room after room, apart from Beeru's. The pahari retired to his quarters, Chacha to his room upstairs.

A strip of light showed under Beeru's closed door. He practised on the piano at night before going to bed. The music pulsed in Kaya's blood, and wove through her heartbeats. *What's come over me, she wondered: What's this restlessness disguised in a thin skin of happiness? She stripped the skin off, and saw a longing turn over inside her. A lump rose in her throat. I've grown up, she told herself. Her eyelids drooped with sleep. Her dry, scaly lips mumbled Beeru, Beeru while she led herself into believing that he might just hear her, although, had he turned up at her door then, she wouldn't have known what to say to him, she'd have even found herself wanting to hide under her quilt. That sound from Beeru's room was like a signpost pointing in no particular direction, yet it seemed to draw her irresistibly. Kaya lay there, under the sign, shivering, her thoughts in turmoil, buffeted by nebulous longings, caught in a kind of storm she had never experienced at home. She sensed that ever since her first day here a golden web had started unfurling about her, a web that reached out all around — the town, the abandoned church, the mountain flowers, and the mysterious hill woman who wore a nose-ring. But, above all, as she was about to sleep there was the sudden, gnawing memory of a body nailed to a swinging piece of wood, radiating intense suffering and agony; it stood near her pillow, utterly silent but pleading.*

What did he die for?

Four

The days were getting shorter, and the sun was barely visible. A pale cloud, neither properly dark nor properly light, covered the town. The air, too, had turned invisible: no longer could it be seen in the rustling of leaves, the stirring of grass; the trees were now leafless and the damp grass wilted in the cold. Leeches basked on the rocks, white against the stone, making the stone seem leprous.

From the chimneys smoke curled upwards all day, swaying like snakes and driving the alarmed migratory birds into the bushes. Kaya heard their desolate cries throughout the day.

Beeru once pointed out such a bird to her.

'It comes from Kashmir', he whispered in her ear.

'From so far away?'

'They stop on the way to rest, of course.'

The bird sat in a deodar tree. Its startled eyes like bright gems, its plumage was brilliant and its long tail like that of an aeroplane.

'It comes every year', Beeru added.

'How do you know it's the same bird?'

'I know — it always sits in this tree.'

It was midday. They were on an abandoned tennis court some way below the house, surrounded by evergreen pines, deodars and oaks. But the only poplar stood stark naked: the mass of leaves on the ground under it had grown thicker with each passing day.

That migrating bird kept screeching continuously, until at dusk it flew out of sight into the wood.

Beeru stood inertly — sometimes it seemed to Kaya that he

came with her every afternoon only to ensure that she wasn't unaccompanied. He didn't seem to need her: he could be alone even when with her. Kaya could not recollect his ever having sought her out on his own, or talking to her about Chacha or that woman who lived in the servants' quarters.

Still, once out of doors, a change came over him and he seemed to unwind in the open air. He would turn into an animated guide, a historian of the house, of its dark corners — the possessor of the key to the mysteries lurking behind the closed doors of a castle. His normally calm eyes would glint feverishly, and then it seemed to Kaya that there were two Beerus — one who kept to his room, withdrawn, aloof, who practised by himself on the piano at night; and the other, this boy among the trees, patiently pointing out astonishing things to her — the leeches and earthworms under rocks, the birds that came from distant lands: things she'd never noticed earlier despite living in these very mountains. Sometimes, he would break into laughter, not at her ignorance (as Lama would), nor out of conceit, but for no obvious reason, as though nothing mattered — yet this laughter was also tinged with a sadness that welded the two Beerus together.

Kaya constantly flitted between these two incarnations of Beeru. When she approached one, the other turned unfamiliar; if she tried to get closer to the unfamiliar, the familiar became hopelessly distant again.

The wire netting that enclosed the tennis court was their usual destination — the finishing line they touched before turning back.

But today Beeru continued past the netting towards the low-roofed, green pavilion. There were broken benches inside with rotting leaves and blades of grass scattered on them.

'This is where they would sit.' Beeru looked at Kaya.

'Whoever would come to this battered-down place?'

'The English children and their nannies. From here they watched the elders play.'

Kaya had followed Beeru into the pavilion and looked around it. A sharp, stale odour filled the air. Bird nests hung from the roof, hard goat pellets were strewn on the floor — and over all these fell a pale light, a frozen glow from the past.

Built by the English long years ago, the tennis court lay abandoned, traces of white-lime lines still visible. The wire netting around it quivered in the dry air.

Where had those people gone?

Kaya stepped out of the pavilion and saw Chacha's house up on the hillside in front. The path below it was lined on either side by oaks and pines, which largely concealed the servants' quarters — of which only the yellow walls were visible.

A bird in the deodar went on screeching.

'Let's rest here for a while', Beeru said behind Kaya.

'No, not here.' Kaya wanted to get away from the strong smell in the pavilion.

The ground fell beyond the tennis court. Dense clusters of trees, bushes, huge rocks — all these seemed to lead straight down to a dark ravine.

The cries of birds had been left behind, but the monotone resonance of cicada sounds wound through the forest.

'See, that's where we went the other day.'

Beeru stopped. Kaya looked up and saw the church, its beams dark with age, looming between two hills opposite them.

'It seems so high from here!' Beeru said.

Kaya was astonished that she had ever been so high up on that hill. The cross outside the church seemed to hover in the clouds like a bird, its wings outstretched. The indolent afternoon sun glinted off the cross.

Kaya sat on a boulder overhung by a branch.

On the other side of the boulder, Beeru looked towards the deep shadows of the wooded hill, its quiet broken by the impatient, plaintive chant of cicadas, which Kaya periodically heard, then lost.

'How do you know?' she asked.

'Know what?'

'That those children sat in the pavilion, that their elders played?'

'I saw it in a photograph.' Beeru laughed gently. 'We've a book at home entitled *Falkland and the Passing Times*. It contains this photograph which shows children with their nannies watching the game.'

Beeru walked round the boulder. Appearing between the low

overhanging branch and the boulder, his face seemed to be sliced in half.

'We must go now.'

'But there's light still', insisted Beeru.

In the feeble light of the wintry afternoon, Kaya saw in a single, startling superimposed image, the quivering netting and the bough overhead and, framed between the two, the abandoned tennis court, pavilion, benches, nests. Something was happening to her that had never happened before. She sat still, aware of Beeru's breath near her, her heart pounding, a yearning in her sere soul.

'You're not disliking being here, are you?' Beeru's voice was low and soft.

'No, Beeru — not any more.'

'You won't run away now?'

'I don't even know the way.'

'Would you, if you knew it?'

'I was only joking. I won't go anywhere.'

Kaya shook her head. Beeru's gaze was entangled in the wire netting. A flight of birds flew down the hill in a dark mass.

'Have you ever been to the servants' quarters, Kaya?'

'Which quarters?'

'Where the pahari lives.'

'No, I haven't', she lied.

'Father hasn't told you anything?'

'About what?'

Beeru looked at her. That familiar melancholic, solemn expression was back in his eyes — and it struck Kaya that she was losing him so soon again, that he was already withdrawing behind his closed doors, slipping away.

Beeru looked away towards the netting where the first shadows of the evening had crept down upon the hill.

'Oh, it's nothing — just an idle question. Let's go now', he said. 'It's time for my music lesson.'

Kaya did not get up. Untruth had now come between them. She wanted to rush in before the door closed. Her heart raced as she attempted to do so, but something pulled her back: *You're a selfish girl, Kaya! You've always been selfish.* She wished she could break free, reach out to him, touch him — but then suddenly she felt as if she had neither hands nor feet, that she could neither move forward nor draw back. There was only this wild thumping in her chest, this flame of longing in an arid desert, a longing she had once seen in Ginny's eyes: Was this what Lama called soul? This clotted thing stuck to the collar of a blood-spattered body — the soul!

'Listen', she said.

'What's it?'

'What was the title of that book?'

'Which book?'

'In which children sat on benches, watching a tennis match.'

'Falkland and the Passing Times.'

'Why not just *Falkland?* Why *the Passing Times?*'

But Beeru had already started walking away towards the tennis court. Perhaps he didn't even hear her.

Kaya heard the bird screech from its perch in the deodar.

There was another sound which Kaya alone heard night after night.

After dinner she'd go back to her room, Chacha to the library, Beeru to his piano.

Before long the piano would fall silent and silence then engulfed the house. She would be on the point of dozing off when she'd hear that sound in the dark, and wake up.

Chacha would look in at her room, then retreat to turn the light off in the library; but Kaya watched him through her open door.

Chacha would then put on his overcoat, pick up a walking-stick, and go down the back stairs, his footsteps echoing for a while.

And then, nothing. Kaya could see nothing. She would listen to the forlorn swish of the wind over chairs on the veranda, across the dark library, behind Beeru's closed door . . . and her imagination would then drift along the path Chacha took through heaped leaves under rustling pines in a winter sky — and throughout she thought she heard the pahari woman's tinkling laughter: *So you came!*

A strange sensation would run through Kaya as she thought of the woman's voice and saw herself hurrying up the steps to her quarters, rattling the door-chain. The woman would open the door at once, as if she had been waiting for her. Her white teeth flashed between full, fleshy lips: *So you came!* She'd be both reassured and nervous on seeing Kaya. In her confusion she'd hold Kaya's hand, release it, shrink into herself, draw back her hands and feet under her clothing. Kaya missed nothing — not those clanking anklets, not those henna-dyed hands red like Kali Ma's, though this woman wore an altogether different face: round, broad, extremely pale from living in the sunless room. The fold of her sari over the back of her head was caught in a hairpin; this hitched-up hanging end bobbed up and down as she nodded. The woman dragged Kaya to the mat in the middle of the room. *So you came*, she'd say again, gazing avidly at Kaya.

Kaya went to see the woman late in the evenings, when Beeru's music lessons were in progress and Chacha out on the Mall. Kaya would be on her own then. In the last hour of the chilly evening, the lone light in the servants' quarters shone like a beacon — and Kaya went over, drawn irresistibly.

This evening the woman's eyes were unusually bright. As soon as she saw Kaya in the doorway she pulled her in by both hands and pressed her lips to Kaya's palms. Her warm, fast breathing, tickled Kaya's hands.

'You won't tell anyone, will you?' the woman said, rolling her eyes like a mischievous child.

Kaya shook her head, breathlessly.

'Not even Beeru?'

'Not even him.'

'You know what Sahib said last night? He said, if I wanted, I could go out with you. Shall we?'

'Alone?' Kaya sounded incredulous.

'Well, not exactly', she laughed. 'There will be the two of us.'

'Where shall we go?'

'We can go to see the waterfall. I've been there before — I know the way.'

'You haven't been on an outing anywhere else after that?'

'No. Not here.' Suddenly her eyes dimmed and she turned pale again. 'Long ago, in our land, I'd roam about the whole day. Then Sahib brought me here. He asked me not to go out anywhere. No errands for me; my son does that. I have only to cook the food. I like this, too — plenty of rest.' She spoke slowly, in short sentences, as if language to her was a mountain stream, to cross which she needed to seek a safe foothold at every short step.

'Isn't your home somewhere near by?'

'Near by?' The woman's nostrils flared. 'Ever heard of Narkanda? It's right at the top. One goes there by bus. When I came here with Sahib I felt dizzy for three days afterwards.'

Kaya raised her head enquiringly.

'Chacha brought you here?' She thought her voice sounded hollow.

'Who else? Could I have ever come by myself? I had this brat who kept howling all the way here. On top of it, I threw up again and again. That was my first bus ride.'

'Why did you come so far away?'

Darkness gathered in the woman's eyes. Neither pain nor anger, not even resentment — nothing there except the darkness that descends in the mountains as quietly as it does in the eyes.

'What could I do? Your Chacha brought me here.'

Kaya started: the word *Chacha* instead of the more formal *Sahib* seemed to brush her lips like a man's touch on a woman's mouth — and she began to tremble. Kaya stared at the woman's feet under her red lehanga, at her henna-bright palms, the parted lips. Her being in the rooms here, and Chacha last night on the stairs outside — somehow this seemed fated: this seemed to have always happened, even before Kaya arrived; it would happen even after Kaya left.

'Come here.' The woman pulled the curtain aside. 'Do you see?'

Kaya drew nearer. She saw two hills leaning against each other, with the valley between them in shadows.

'Beyond the hill, beyond those two hills, way up in the range, is Narkanda.'

'That's where you came from?'

'You can't see it for the clouds', she said in a distant voice, daydreaming like those drowsy hills.

'You must miss your home.'

'Not really — I had no one there.' She paused for a moment, then resumed dreamily: 'But when the wind blows I remember the apple orchards. The apples would plop to the ground in the wind!'

Her dupatta had slipped off her bosom, and the hairpin hung loose. Her eyes were shot with filaments of red — like thread strewn on the floor around a sewing machine.

She turned away from the door, and sat on the bed, yawned and stretched, her body exposed through her clothes. Her lehanga hiked up, and the white legs, whiter than her face, were openly visible.

'Why are you staring at me?' She laughed, pulling Kaya near herself.

Kaya warmed to her touch, but felt slightly confused.

'Did Chacha speak to you?' the woman asked.

'About what?'

'About me, of course.'

'No.'

'And his son?' Her lips curled in contempt.

'Who — Beeru?' Kaya grew apprehensive. 'He doesn't know anything.'

'He does. He thinks I'm a sorceress.' She laughed drily. 'He thinks I've cast a spell on his father. . . . Tell me, do I look like a sorceress to you?' She fixed Kaya in her troubled gaze.

'Doesn't he ever come here?'

'Isn't it enough that his father does?'

What was it in the woman's tone that made Kaya tremble? She wanted to flee but sat there huddled, in the grip of a terror and an unknown attraction, even as the woman looked out towards the mountains, the westerly sun caught in her nose-ring, a barbed smile on her lips, lost and lonely, oblivious of her loneliness, of the cold — a hill woman, the woman with the nose-ring, or just an unreal dream that hovered day and night over Falkland.

'Kaya, you'd better go. It's getting dark.'

'Yes, I think I must get along.' Kaya rose to leave.

'Listen', she called after Kaya.

Kaya turned to her where she sat on the bed.

'Come here.'

Kaya went back to her. The woman clasped her shoulders, looking deep into Kaya's eyes.

'You're a good girl, Kaya.'

Kaya merely stared back.

'You've been a great comfort to me.' She sounded frightened, as if affected by the gathering darkness.

'Look at me!'

Kaya met her eyes.

'Do you think I'm a sorceress?'

They stared at each other in the dimming light.

There was some noise outside and the woman let go of Kaya. Someone was coming up the stairs at a run.

'They're looking for you everywhere.'

The pahari was gasping for breath. His gaze swung from Kaya to his mother and back. It seemed to Kaya that he'd run here all the way.

'Who's looking?'

'There's a man at the house. Looks like a Tibetan mendicant to me — quite like a beggar, but he asked to see you.'

'You sure he asked to see *me*?'

'Of course!' There was no doubt in his mind. 'He's wearing two pigtails; his legs are wrapped in puttees. When he walks his anklets clank.'

Kaya pushed past the pahari towards the stairs without another glance at the woman.

She broke into a run.

The trees whirled overhead.

Mangtu was waiting on the bottom stair. On seeing Kaya he held his arms out wide. Kaya ran into them. A hurt, frightened dove, she clung to him, her heart clamouring in her ears.

'Well, well!' Mangtu stroked her tousled head, her dusty, grimy hair. He had no words to console her. 'Well, well', he repeated helplessly. 'Don't you bathe, girl? Look at all this dirt!'

But for the moment Kaya was bathing in Mangtu's smell, rich with memories of home, their kitchen, his room.

'Is everything all right at home?'

'Yes, yes, everything's fine', said Mangtu. 'There was a letter from Babu', he continued after a while, slowly, as if wringing each word of its meaning. Kaya watched him anxiously: something might yet come of those words — some reassurance, some hope — that might sustain her through the rest of her days here.

'Babu wrote to say that he'd gone to Meerut for a day. He met Lama there. She was asking after you.'

In the wan light the words 'Meerut' and 'Lama' appeared to Kaya like creatures from another planet that she'd heard about ages ago, long since dead, whose spirits still roamed the hills day and night.

'I met the young Sahib just now. He took me to your room. You must be lonely in it.'

Kaya nodded.

'You aren't frightened, are you? The house is so big.'

'It's all right.'

'Anyway,' Mangtu sucked his breath, 'Babu will be here soon.'

'That letter — what else did it say?' Kaya's lips quivered, her body went numb, her gaze swam.

'What more need you know? Isn't it enough that Babu will soon be home? As it is, Mother has been alone too long already.'

'Why, isn't Bua there?'

'Didn't I tell you? She left the third day after you came here. She said her muscles hurt in the cold.' Mangtu had an air of self-satisfaction about him. 'Well, you can't expect a plainswoman to weather the mountain cold, can you?'

So Mother was alone in the house, alone with Chhote. In her mind's eye she saw Mother sitting on the veranda, looking out over Hilta Hills, with the wind sweeping through the empty rooms behind her.

'Where does Chhote sleep?'

'In Mother's bedroom. Your room has been locked up.' Mangtu blinked, turning his eyes past Kaya to the jagged skyline where the sun was beginning to go down, plunging the hills in darkness; but in the east the light still shimmered like quicksilver on the peaks. A pall of eerie silence stretched over the town below.

'Did it snow there?'

'You must be crazy! If it snowed there, would it remain dry hereabouts?' The bones in Mangtu's chest crackled as he sighed. He looked squarely at Kaya. 'What's the matter? Aren't you happy here?'

'I'm perfectly happy.' Kaya took a firm grip on herself. 'You can tell Mother I don't miss home at all.'

Mangtu peered at her uncertainly.

'That's what Chacha said, too', he observed.

'What did he say?' Kaya had a sinking sensation.

'He said you keep so quiet nobody can even make out that you're in the house. Now, Mother would hardly believe that! Remember how you'd get under Memsahib's skin?'

'Mrs Joshua?'

'She can't even walk now, poor thing! She comes out only to collect her newspaper.'

'Mangtu, is it true that an eye stares out from the back of the letter-box?'

'Back of what?' Mangtu looked at her suspiciously.

'The letter-box — when it's empty.'

'How absurd of you to think that, Kaya!'

Mangtu took off his cap and examined it before dusting it on his knees. He was wearing a frayed khaki overcoat. In that coat, and with the torn strips of clothing swathing his legs, he looked rather like an old wounded soldier. His feet were clad in dusty sackcloth instead of shoes.

He removed a bag from his shoulder and opened it with raw fingers to take out two boxes, one big, another small.

'Look,' he said, 'this bigger box is full of muttris. In the other there is a cake Memsahib sent for you — don't eat it if it's stale. . . . And now I must set off.'

'Can't you stay for the night?'

'We've to think of Mother too. She'd be alone.'

Mangtu straightened up. A patch of sunlight still hung to the wall. Above, a pale half-moon, like a slice of an apple, awaited the night. He mumbled something under his breath — about his aching legs perhaps, or about Mother or Babu's visit — and picked up his bag.

Kaya stood with the two boxes clutched to her chest.

'Any message for Mother?'

Nothing! Nothing at all! Kaya shook her head violently, shrinking, as if sensing some primal danger, to the single point of a heartbeat. The rest of her body went numb. Her eyes followed sightlessly the roads which in a hill town plunge deep and rise steeply again like a game of snakes and ladders. She watched Mangtu walk up the path until he was a mere smudge. She put the boxes down on the bottom step and ran after him, where he could be seen among the trees touched by the last rays of the sun. Soon he vanished behind a bend in the path. Kaya ran among the bushes below the servants' quarters, trying desperately to protect her legs from thorns. Mangtu reappeared, a doll conjured by magic, further along the path before the trees concealed him again. Kaya ran as far as she could. In those last moments she could see only his back, his overcoat flapping in the wind, in which he looked like some huge bird, strutting about, wings spread. Kaya pulled up helplessly when she saw him turn into the road beyond the oak displaying the Falkland sign at the end of the path. For a while she stood still, then began to scream. She fell silent just as abruptly, frightened by the sound of her own voice.

When Kaya returned to the house she found the two boxes still on the step, lying in the soft glow of the sinking sun.

Kaya sank on the edge of her bed. Her head was in a whirl, her eyes swam with the walls. In another moment the walls stood firm, and her gaze steadied. So did her pain. She had a strange, overwhelming feeling of time flowing on. No one in the house — not Beeru at his piano, not Chacha in the library, not the

woman with the nose-ring in the quarters — seemed aware that
when everything inside one goes still, time begins to flow: not
the time of clocks, which had no significance for Kaya — but the
other kind which rolled out like a ball of wool at each tug of a
pair of knitting needles. Kaya sensed this tugging within her. The
scream which had welled up in the bushes when she chased after
Mangtu was not entirely powerless; like a pickaxe, it struck chips
off the frozen heap of years, baring oozy undersurfaces. One
good blow, one scream, one nightmare, was all it took to thaw
it. As Kaya sat on her bed, she sensed something flowing inside
her, float, melt into a lava of anger and hate, of longings bitter
as gall, of attachment, of illusions she seemed to have been born
with, whose onus she had borne to this day, to this winter evening
in her room where she sat eyeing the two boxes Mangtu had left
with her.

Kaya got up, as if it was necessary to go out in order to reach
within. It was dark outside. Last year when it snowed, Chhote
and she shovelled it off Mrs Joshua's doorstep. No one had
seemed to care then about the snow piling round deserted
houses. Gradually the snow piled all over them. Does this
happen to people too? Snow buries them too, doesn't it, because
no one comes forward to clear it off in time. They go under,
finished forever, as if they had never existed — and the screams
that surge from deep within return off the walls of snow: no
one outside can hear them even if they try.

There was a slight rumbling noise. Kaya leaned out from
her window. She saw what looked like a line of glow-worms
snaking its way along the hills below, now visible here, now
gone behind the hill to reappear on the other side: it was the
Simla-Kalka shuttle, each small compartment lighted. The train
vanished from sight periodically, as if swallowed by the hills.
Then, as it reappeared nearer, it seemed to leap out like an
image from a cinema screen. As the hills shook Kaya recoiled
from the window, but when she looked again a little later the
hills were back in place, and the light had moved on. But the
distant rumble of the wheels could still be heard, and sparks
flew down the last hill, towards Kalka. Then there was nothing
more to see.

Kaya let her head fall on the window-frame and started weeping helplessly, without knowing why she was weeping. The tears sprang from no known source and coursed towards no known goal, and soon left no trace either.

Kaya pulled away from the window with a start. She thought she heard someone stealthily approach her in the darkness.

'Is that you, Lama?'

'I was passing by when I saw you at the window.'

Kaya turned round. The half moon shone on Lama's face as she stood in the shadows between Kaya's room and the library.

'What were you doing in the dark?'

'I was watching the train.'

Kaya started across the room, then stopped. It seemed that something had just moved in the space between the two of them: was it the soul? Moving from pain to happiness and towards Lama, from round Lama's feet back to Kaya's tear-stained cheeks, down across the lump deep between her breasts — touching, rubbing, pinching — as she did, ages ago on the gallery to impress Kali Ma — naked, shivering in the cold air, intoxicated, gone mad . . .

'Lama, can you hear me?'

'What's it, Kaya? I'm here.'

'Can't you please stop this?'

She reached out to grasp Lama's hand. Lama came over unresisting.

'Look here, can't you stop this, please?'

Lama turned her calm eyes to where Kaya was pointing on the bare floor.

There was only a pale sliver of moonlight there.

Kaya stared at it, without blinking. Then she looked around her. She could see no one there any more. She was alone in the middle of the dark room.

Five

'Have you seen Baba anywhere?'

'Who?' Kaya looked up.

'Beeru Baba', the pahari repeated, looking into her face. 'Do you know if he's back?'

'Why, isn't he in his room?'

'No, he isn't there.' He looked a trifle worried. 'He'd gone out to the music teacher's and isn't back yet.'

Kaya said nothing.

The pahari was in a hurry and ran to the servants' quarters.

Kaya went to the veranda. It was cold there, and she hugged herself, shivering, wondering why Beeru was out so late. She sensed that he had begun keeping a distance from her. His solitary light continued to burn till well into the night and once she'd thought of going to see him, but his door was closed. There was so deep a silence behind it that she did not even knock, and retraced her steps.

The veranda had been emptied of chairs. The sky was a perfect blue, yet it could snow any day. They were now in early December when the air is crystal-clear. The sky shone through like a gem, blue, solid, cold, set against the hills over which thin fluffy clouds drifted.

Kaya watched the cloud intently. *No, these don't look like snow-bearing clouds*, she told herself.

Beeru's chair was empty at dinner-time. The pahari served them hot chapattis. He still looked a little worried, unlike Chacha who concentrated on his food.

'Beeru hasn't come in yet', said Kaya, looking up. Chacha nodded indifferently.

'He might have been held up at the music tutor's.'

'Where does he live?'

'In Sanjauli. Not very far from here.'

'Where there's a big cemetery, isn't it?'

'Yes, a cemetery.' Chacha looked at Kaya with curiosity, and his gaze lingered. 'You've been there?'

'No.' Kaya clammed up: she found it impossible to tell Chacha what Mrs Joshua had told her.

'A very old cemetery, indeed', said Chacha. 'It goes back to the days when the English founded this hill town.' He looked over Kaya's head towards the brazier, and said with a smile, 'There are graves here too, you know?'

'Here? In the house?' Kaya shuddered.

'Well, not in the house — not exactly.' The smile still flickered on Chacha's lips, though not in his eyes, which held a glacial stare.

'Have you been to the tennis court yet?' Chacha asked after a while.

'Beeru took me there once.'

'There's tall grass on the slope beyond it. Below that, there are two graves, not readily noticeable — but they once kept prospective tenants away.'

'Two graves?' Kaya asked in alarm, very interested, a fish entangled in the net of Chacha's words.

'One is of the man who built this house, the other of his dog.'

'But why?'

'Why, what?' Chacha's eyes met Kaya's.

Kaya wanted to ask him about the dog and its master, but she was suddenly overcome by sadness.

'And you still took the house?'

'Two ordinary graves — what's there to be afraid of? This house stands on top of the hill, high above the town. I can't comment about ghosts, but at least flies and mosquitoes don't come here.'

But Chachi died in this house, didn't she, Kaya thought to herself. Bua had told her about Chachi. The room in which Kaya was now lodged had belonged to her; her tin trunks still lay under the beds.

Chacha never talked about her, though.

When the pahari came in to collect the plates from the table, he found them both unusually quiet. The silence in the room was broken only by the tiny, crackling explosions of live coals in the dying fire.

Chacha leaned over the table after the pahari had left.

'Kaya,' he said with a slight tremor, 'have you been going to the servants' quarters?'

Kaya was suddenly frightened: had that woman with the nose-ring told on her? She quietly looked at the tabletop.

'I'm . . . I'm very glad that you go to see her.'

With his broad shoulders and long limbs Chacha was a big man, and not a hair in his head had yet turned grey — but at that moment Kaya saw a shadow of frailty stretch across his face.

'Chacha, can't she come into the house?'

Chacha laughed gently, dismissively — the way Beeru would, thought Kaya with a pang. The same quiet gloom, above pain or sorrow or want, was gathering on his face.

'Sometimes it seems you've always been with us.' Chacha's gaze wandered back to the fire. 'I forget that you have to go some day.'

Chacha's words hurt her a little. Hadn't she herself forgotten? In the beginning she kept count of the days left for her departure. She had long stopped doing that, and was not expectantly awaiting the day when she would leave: she was easy here, with day following day, the night, and another day. The thought frightened her now. Perhaps something strange, something she didn't quite understand, was happening to her, as though someone from behind had clamped fingers over her eyes and she didn't know who it was, her heart beating in hope and terror.

Indeed, whose hands had closed over her eyes — Beeru's, or the woman with a nose-ring, or Chacha's? Or no one's? Was the darkness her own creation?

Kaya started as a crackling ember landed in front of her. Chacha rose and, holding it with tongs, put it back in the brazier. Instead of going back to his chair he then stood still, listening to something.

'Did you hear?' he asked keenly.

Kaya thought Beeru might be coming in, but there was no one at the door. Nor were there any footsteps on the stairs. Silence lay thick across the veranda as on any other night.

'That's the waterfall — we can hear it on some nights.'

Was it the same waterfall the woman with the nose-ring was talking about the other afternoon?

'Let's go out. We can hear it better from the veranda.'

Chacha's eyes lit up with an excitement that often possesses people in the mountains — people who have been too long alone — almost to the point of madness.

Kaya had seen such a light in Mrs Joshua's eyes, too.

'Take this — it's cold outside.' Chacha peeled off his shawl to drape it over Kaya's head, her shoulders and chest. He stepped back, saw Kaya bundled from head to toe peering from the folds of the shawl, and laughed. 'You look like a member of the Ku Klux Klan in that!'

He almost dragged Kaya across the room. The moment he opened the door to the veranda a chill draught seemed to penetrate through to Kaya's bones. As the curtain over the door billowed, its shadow surged across the veranda to the trees beyond.

Out there, Chacha looked like the captain on the deck of his ship.

The night was cold and radiant with a full-moon suspended like a lantern above the mountains. The fog in the valley parted before the moonlight to reveal the vaulting heads of trees.

They stood together by the railing.

'Can you hear?' Chacha put his hand on Kaya's shoulder.

Kaya was shivering under the shawl. She pricked her ears, her eyes drooped with the effort of concentration. She didn't hear any well-defined sounds — only a dull, distant rumble breaking upon the darkness in a hazy rhythm, a whisper swelling like a sigh through the moaning woods.

'It's strange, Kaya!' Chacha said quietly. 'Take this view. Those peaks, the wooded hillsides, the clumps of trees — these seem to open up on summer nights: the whole space comes alive then, you can even hear it breathe. Quite unlike the winter: it's frightening at this time.'

He paused as if searching for the proper word. Then he gave up and turned to Kaya, a vacant, distant look in his eyes. In the pale moonlight, he seemed a changed person, lost, lonely, a creature from another planet.

'When I was in the army,' he went on very softly, 'we'd often go hunting on holidays. When we ran into an animal I remember how it would stop in its tracks, absolutely still for a moment, rapt, as if it were waiting for us. It seemed eerie. It's the same with these trees, this grass; these seem to be waiting, too, with bated breath. Look, not a leaf stirs! In silence such as this we hear the waterfall — did you hear it, Kaya?'

It seemed he was talking to himself and Kaya heard him as if through sleep. Leaning on the railing, she caught only scraps of his mumbled words. The wire-netting around the tennis court glimmered faintly below. The tops of pine, deodar and oak were laced with mist. There was a breeze now, and the silver blades of the tall grass swayed. Somewhere beneath it were the two graves in which rested, side by side, the man and his dog. Suddenly, then, it struck Kaya that she had at last fathomed and could almost name the gloom in Chacha's laughter, a name that had time and again eluded her, receding beyond her grasp only to return and haunt her later. The undulating grass over the graves, she realized, was the gloom in Chacha's laughter: she would hold that secret now in her hands if only she dared catch it. But when Kaya raised her head from the railing she knew it had eluded her again after all. It was nowhere now, yet everywhere — in the stir of the grass, on the branches of trees, everywhere. She looked out forlornly into the distance where the peaks reared out of the mist, staring back hard at her . . .

Kaya missed a heartbeat as she saw a shadow tread the leaves along the path below. 'Beeru', she whispered in a thin voice.

'What's it, Kaya? Who's there . . . who's waiting?' said Chacha.

No one. No one was there. Kaya wasn't sure that she had seen Beeru's shadow under the rustling trees. It could have been a jackal or some other animal. Besides, on moonlit nights even the shadows of trees seemed to shift.

That night Chacha didn't go to the servants' quarters. He took his time over his drink in the library. The flush of excitement that Kaya had seen a moment ago on his face had faded: he looked old and weary, and spent. From her bed Kaya saw him get up and slowly walk to the door of her room.

'Are you asleep?'

'No, Chacha.' She sat up at once.

'I'm going upstairs. Could you open the door for Beeru when he comes?'

Chacha's footsteps were audible as he climbed up the steps leading off from the sitting room. The stairs, not visible from outside, had always intrigued Kaya, for to her they suggested a house within a house.

The house soon sank into silence, the wind whistling around it, the jackals whining. There were occasional faint scraping or crawling sounds on the tin roof, which reminded Kaya of flying-foxes that jump from the trees on to roofs at night and return to the trees at daybreak. Whenever Kaya woke at night, the soft scuffing, slurred noises of bats — a dreadful sight by day — caught her attention. She wondered then if they, huddled on the roof, could overhear her breathing, just as she overheard their muffled snorts when lying in bed with her quilt pulled over . . .

But this was a different sound. Kaya started. Someone was knocking on the outer door persistently but gently.

She stepped into the library. The light in it was still on but the fire had died down. She walked across the dining room, towards where the moonlight picked out the notice on the glass pane: *Attention Please — Steps Ahead.*

As Kaya pulled open the outer door, she came up face to face with Beeru.

'You certainly took your time — half an hour!' Beeru looked into her face. 'Had you gone to sleep, or what?'

Kaya moved aside to let him in. He cast about the empty ground floor, dark but for the light in the library.

'Hasn't Papa come back?'

'From where?'

Beeru threw Kaya a searching glance.

'He's upstairs — in his room.'

'At this hour?' Surprised, he looked at the darkened stairs. The door above was closed.

'Had you fallen asleep?' He asked again.

'No.' Kaya shook her head. 'But where were you?'

Beeru's face had turned red in the cold: two spots of colour stood out on his cheekbones. Specks of grass stuck to his brown pullover, and his trousers were rolled up above mud-stained socks.

'I can hardly stand, Kaya.'

'Come, let me take you to your room.'

She took Beeru's hand, clenched and clammy, into hers. He withdrew it. 'No! I can manage', he insisted. He stopped outside his door, and looked round.

'Will you be going to bed now?' Beeru asked.

'Why, is there anything you want?' Kaya took a step towards him.

'I'm feeling slightly strange — both hot and cold by turns.'

'Wait, I'll open the door for you.'

Kaya went into the room and turned on the light. He flopped down on his bed.

'Don't you want to change?'

Beeru lay face down, his legs hanging over the bed, arms on either side of his head which he tossed about.

'Go now, Kaya. I'll soon get to sleep.'

'Yes, I'll go.'

Kaya looked around the cold room. The fire the pahari lit in the evening had gone out, but some live coals still glared through the ashes. When Kaya poked them with the tongs a flame leapt up. Even as she recoiled in alarm, a hope revived that the fire could be got going again. She pushed the half-burnt coal and faggots from the back to the front just as the pahari had taught her. Soon the flames began to dance, and Kaya stood still in amazement. When she turned round she saw Beeru changing into his night-clothes. She saw his back, white, utterly white, in the glow of the fire, with his spine, full and downy, plunging straight down in the middle. She averted her eyes, and resumed prodding the fire vigorously.

'Kaya . . .'

The tongs in Kaya's hand hovered over the fire.

'It's all right — I'm off to my room.'

'Listen, can't you stay for a while?'

Kaya turned to see Beeru in bed with the quilt pulled up to his wet eyes, his face flushed. Seeing Kaya look at the hand-towel beside him, he said slowly: 'I've caught a cold. All my handkerchiefs are used up.'

Kaya stood around uncertainly. I must leave, she told herself firmly — but her feet were riveted to where she stood, her eyes were fixed elsewhere.

'Sit here.' Beeru drew his feet up to make room for her on the bed. The stool was already occupied by his knitting things, balls of wool, a completed sock, the start of another threaded on the needles.

'I feel so hot — is it really that warm?'

Sweat glistened on his forehead.

'Where did you go, Beeru?'

'I didn't go anywhere.'

'Won't you tell me?'

Beeru lowered his head on the pillow. 'I went to the church.'

'So late?'

'I hide inside sometimes, watching for anyone who might walk in.'

Kaya couldn't understand why anyone would go to those ruins at night. 'Who walks in, Beeru?'

'They come to steal the wood', he said. 'Didn't you see how half the church is gone?'

'But what do you do there?' Kaya was frightened by his feverish manner. She hadn't heard him talk so much so willingly before.

'I stand in the alcove — you've seen it.'

Kaya's was astonished. 'Alcove? Doesn't it scare you?'

'No, and I scare them away.' He smiled, again surprising Kaya.

'I don't believe you.' Kaya dared him, trying at the same time to overcome her own fear.

'Really, you should see how they flee when I intone from my hiding place, "I am Jesus, I am watching you." They drop the pried-out planks at once and vanish.'

For all his excitement, Beeru spoke in a monotone, the doleful, lost, inward look back in his eyes — in which everything left a lingering signal or mark.

For whom did Beeru do this? What beckoned to him?

Kaya recalled dimly the wooden truss in the alcove with the drooping figure of a man nailed to it.

The chimney crackled with smoke from the fireplace, as though someone was sitting in it and coughing.

Beeru pushed himself on to his elbows to retrieve his red notebook from the piano-top. He slipped it under his pillow.

'What's that, Beeru?' asked Kaya, her curiosity aroused.

'A diary. I write in it every day.'

'What do you write about?'

'About myself. Papa says I should record my day-to-day life regularly — like a newspaper.'

His lashes cast shadows on his flushed face.

'You never told me.'

'Do you tell me everything?' His voice trembled slightly.

'What everything?'

'Where do you go every evening?'

Kaya felt her lips go dry. Her eyes smarted from the smoke.

'You saw me?'

'Well, I know.'

Suddenly Beeru looked away, as if mortally afraid of what Kaya might have to say after all. Even if one knows that others know our terrible secret, one yet prays that it remains unexposed — it might in time turn out to be unreal, fade away, die a natural death.

'So you know where I go?'

Kaya wanted to draw Beeru into the arena of her heartbeat, but he kept quiet, his face to the wall.

'Don't you ever go there yourself, Beeru?'

Kaya took another step towards him; if he was reluctant to come nearer her secret, she would meet his fear.

'No.' Beeru shook his head. 'It's a bad place.'

'But your Papa goes there, doesn't he?' Kaya was carried away on a wave of cruelty.

Beeru looked at Kaya desolately. Nevertheless, he held on to good sense and withdrew discreetly behind the barriers he had built around himself.

'I know that. Perhaps he'll yet see through it.' He spoke in a dry, level voice, like one whose mind was made up, who would not let anything on earth make him budge from his position.

Kaya sensed then a stirring within her, of a bleak longing, to reach out to Beeru, to place her hand on his sad, burning face and see for herself — but see what? His head on the pillow, Beeru looked as distant as the idol of Kali — speechless, stony-eyed, a block of stone.

Her hand lay on Beeru's quilt. He seemed to have drifted off to sleep. His narrow chest rose and fell, now evenly, now quivering, his wheezing breath in a tangle.

Kaya rose quietly. Beeru opened his eyes.

'Go back to sleep,' she said, 'I'll turn off the light.'

'Are you leaving?' Beeru held her in his gaze. His face, flushed red a while ago, had turned pale. Stray hair was plastered to his damp forehead.

'Is it very hot?' she asked.

'No,' he said with a wan smile, 'it's chilly . . . listen, there must be a spare blanket where you were sitting.'

Kaya took the blanket and tucked it round him up to his chin. He looked on gratefully: in gratitude, sometimes words fail to assume form; they melt away instead.

'You'd should go now, Kaya.' He closed his eyes. 'I already feel much better.'

She did not move from his bedside.

'Beeru . . . '

He opened his eyes.

'Did you come by the bridle path near the tennis court tonight?'

'No, I didn't. But why do you ask?'

Kaya stood still even as a shudder ran down her lean frame.

'Never mind.'

She turned away, flicked off the light, and left.

As Kaya lay in bed that night she continued to listen for a long time to the flying-foxes crawl on the tin roof above. Then, as her eyes filled with sleep, she saw Beeru's open eyes, his gaze swimming, the eyeballs afloat. As she sank deeper into slumber, she lost sight of the eyeballs. Instead, she saw a naked white back rippling like a fish. That naked back — where had she seen it? She bent forward, her hand outstretched, to touch it. Someone spun her about. 'Kaya, *Orré* Kaya, you wretch!' Chhote called out to her, waving both his hands, not empty but clasping something that had black feathers, that was crying out to be set free. 'Look here, open your hands! Let go!' Kaya strode up to Chhote to prise open his fists . . . and then what flew up out of his grasp was not a bird, nor a flying-fox, but Ginny — yes, Ginny — with shiny pinions: it escaped past Kaya's shoulder with short, sharp, squeaky yelps into thin air.

Kaya drew a breath, and turned over on her side. A moonbeam tripping in through the window came to sit by her tired, troubled head.

Six

Kaya gathered her skirt at the knees. The hill, thick with bushes, fell off beyond the tennis court. The hem of her dress caught on a branch. She looked up, and saw red-blossomed darhu shrubs bearing small pomegranate-like fruit . . . and the flaming-red lehanga of the woman with the nose-ring and henna-dyed feet.

The woman's anklets jangled ahead, and Kaya hurried after that sound.

Mist rose from the ravine they descended into. Kaya gasped as stinging-nettle brushed her leg. She sat down, wishing she could stretch out right there on the wet grass. A pale sheet of sunlight was wedged between the clouds above and the fog below. Some bare trees added to the forlorn winter scene.

Kaya pulled herself to her feet and ran to catch up with the woman. The woman's kohl-rimmed eyes watched her disapprovingly: 'Rest if you must, but why stop again and again?'

'How far is it now?' asked Kaya panting, her eyes watering from the icy wind.

'Not very far, I think. I've been here only once before.'

They set off down the path again. Suddenly the woman gripped Kaya's shoulder: 'Look, that's our house up there!'

Kaya threw her head back, her heart thumping against her ribs. The fog clung to the gallery, Chacha's room stuck out above the empty veranda, Beeru's lay below to the right. Beeru must be in his bed by the window, surrounded by his balls of wool and knitting needles, his notebook bound in red atop the piano. . . . What does he write about in that notebook?

But what was she doing here in this forest? Even as her thoughts turned to the house above, Kaya heard the woman's voice behind her: 'Your head will spin if you keep looking up.'

Sure enough, the sky above, the clouds above the trees, and even Beeru's window went into a whirl. She had not seen Beeru since that night. He had not left his room, and Kaya had not heard the piano recently. Chacha paced the floor all day, and only a stranger, the doctor, entered Beeru's room. When he came out and talked with Chacha, Kaya, hovering near by, would hurriedly retreat to her room.

Kaya had plenty of free time on her hands. She could do what she wanted, go where she pleased.

'You idle around the house all day — why don't you come out with me?' the woman insisted, trying to pin Kaya down to her promise.

'Where?'

'Didn't you want to see the waterfall before going back?'

Yes, of course. She'd see all there was to see before going back. She was free. She could go anywhere.

The woman laughed, ruffling Kaya's hair.

'What are you gaping at? Come, let's go on.'

The woman led the way. Sorceress — that's what Beeru called her. What she says, happens. Nothing escapes her — not the trees, not the sky, not the bushes.

Not even Chacha — the thought terrified Kaya. She fell in step behind the woman, picking her way carefully down the rocky slope. Yet her shoes repeatedly got stuck in the stones, bleached, water-worn, and her heels burned despite the cold. Fog stretched over the trees, but the sun filtered through to dapple the path, bits of grass on stones, the fallen pine-needles.

'Wait a minute! Can you hear anything?' The woman took Kaya's hand.

Kaya heard nothing — except the faint crackle of a branch as a bird flew off. Then the stillness returned, loud with the sound of cicadas.

'The stream's just ahead.'

'Where?' asked Kaya.

'Can't you hear it, girl? You can't expect it to come looking for you!'

This time Kaya heard a faint rumble, as of rolling clouds. But the next moment she was distracted by an intoxicating scent that rose not from the wood or the soil but from the woman with the nose-ring. Kaya's pulse throbbed, and she felt uneasy.

'What's the matter with you?' The woman gripped Kaya's hand.

'Nothing. Don't you think we should move on?'

'Why are you trembling?'

'It's the cold.' Kaya broke away, and walked ahead.

What was she doing in this forest? With this woman?

Kaya walked alone for a while. One doesn't feel lonely in a forest, she thought: every bush or tree seems to hide someone. Beeru's eyes had always reminded Kaya of forests. The forest around her now seemed to be peopled with watching eyes.

She stopped where the path split, one offshoot climbing up the hill, the other going further down. Between the two stood an old weather-beaten signboard with blurred letters. *To the Falls*, it said, without pointing in any particular direction.

'Follow that track downwards', said the woman behind her. 'Why must you stop all the time?'

Kaya took a deep breath. She noticed a mole on the woman's upper lip. How beautiful she looked, thought Kaya — how different from that homely, pale-looking creature within the four walls of her room: she seemed to have grown younger out here in the open.

On the way down, the bushes constantly caught at Kaya's skirt. The woman burst out laughing. 'You silly girl, this way you'll soon reduce your skirt to tatters.' She extricated Kaya from the thorns, letting her gaze travel up Kaya's legs to her small breasts. Then she picked up a stone and brought it heavily down on a darhu-pomegranate. Its juice flowed over her hand. 'Look, blood — blood is running down my fingers!' The Japanese-doll eyes in the hill woman's round, pale face flickered. It really looked like blood, Kaya thought; seeing it her own blood churned, cramping her insides, knocking on the door of her being — as if it could hardly wait to flow out in a flood.

Ahead was a small bridge of felled trees across a thin stream that gushed down on white pointed rocks with a hammer-like sound. This was hardly a waterfall, thought Kaya, it's only a modest mountain stream.

'Could you wait a moment?' said the woman; 'I'll wash my hands. They're so sticky — just touch them!'

She held out her hands. The 'blood' had dried. Kaya did not touch it and looked at the woman intently.

'We won't go any further, will we?' asked Kaya.

'Exhausted, are you?' She did not laugh this time — just stared at Kaya before going down towards the bridge.

The trees on either side met overhead, forming a roof. As a breeze sprang up, a patch of sky showed through the rustling foliage, but the branches soon resumed their embrace as the breeze subsided.

Kaya sat on a boulder. Pine needles and cones were scattered everywhere. The breeze had abated. Nothing seemed to move except the stream. There was not a sound.

Not a sound. So when Kaya heard the splash of hands in running water, it seemed to be an aberration, just another aspect of the jungle's silence, one that made the silence even deeper.

'Do you want to wash?' The woman was with Kaya again.

'No.' Kaya shook her head. She did not dare go too near the stream: the sight of running water, even in an innocuous brook, always made her dizzy.

The woman lay on the pine-needles, propping her head on her elbow and looking at Kaya. 'Have you gone to sleep?'

'No.' Kaya looked straight at the clouds coasting above the thatch of entangled branches.

'You hardly sleep at night — what do you do on the gallery?'

A stray cloud clogged Kaya's eyes with an endless grey. She blinked.

'When I first came here,' said the woman, 'I too found it difficult to sleep. I'd lie awake, listening the whole night to the dreary silence of the woods.'

Kaya lowered her eyes at the woman's tone — dull, hard, without pity.

'You pity me, Kaya?'

'What for?'

'No,' the woman laughed, 'you don't know me well enough, do you? It must be Chacha or that poor boy Beeru whom you pity!'

Was it disgust, contempt, or just plain unconcern in the woman's voice?

Kaya got off the boulder and sat on the grass opposite the reclining woman.

'Have you ever seen a dead body, Kaya?'

Kaya's mind wandered off — Ginny, the misshapen lump between Mother's thighs . . . no, no, they weren't dead, they weren't human! Kaya looked around in a daze: the dismal light, the chattering stream as it splashed upon the rocks, the woman — her dupatta fallen away from her full, heaving breasts — sprawled out beside her.

'You haven't? Nor had I,' the woman spoke in a lowered voice, 'until my husband died.'

'Your husband?'

The woman raised her head. The nose-ring quivered, her lips parted, the forehead creased.

'I don't have pity for anyone now.'

'Which husband?'

'That night when they took him away to be burnt, I had a bath — and a good look at the marks he'd left on my back. You want to have a look, too, Kaya? The marks are still there.'

The woman unbuttoned her kameez. She was wearing a woollen vest under it. She peeled them both off her back — so white, but crisscrossed from one breast to the other by bluish weals, which glimmered, almost like railway tracks, in the dull light of the cloudy afternoon.

'Come on, feel them!'

The woman drew Kaya's hand over to the welts on her back.

'Here, feel them! The man is dead, but his marks are still there.'

Kaya had difficulty breathing. She felt she was crumbling under the woman's touch. The golden-yellow disc of the waning afternoon sun emerged from the clouds to scatter through over-hanging branches in copperish-red spots on the woman's naked back. Kaya withdrew her hand. The woman still lay on her stomach, breathing deeply. Then she rolled over on to her back. Her hair came undone, the nose-ring glinted in the sun, her lehanga rode up above her knees, her legs opened out like a pair of scissors. The silver anklets on her feet were caked with mud.

The woman stroked Kaya's cheeks gently.

'Silly girl', she said in a barely audible whisper. 'Did I frighten you?' She laughed soundlessly, her eyes taking in Kaya. 'It seems you know nothing. Tell me, do you bleed?'

Kaya's eyes widened.

'What do you mean?'

'Just what I said — bleed, don't you? Foul, like darhu juice.' Her lips were still parted in a silent laugh. 'So you've seen nothing yet — neither a dead man nor your own blood.'

The woman drew her knees up. Her anklets clanked. A bird took off screeching from a bush; it fluttered away along the stream.

'Your servant came for you, didn't he?'

'Who? Mangtu?' Kaya looked at the woman.

'I thought you'd go home with him.'

'Won't you go back, too?'

The woman's tired eyes rested on Kaya.

Kaya's heart went out to her now.

'Back to your own home — won't you?' said Kaya as if to console her.

'With whom?'

'With Chacha, of course! It was he who brought you here.'

'Either you know nothing or you pretend, Kaya. I'll not go anywhere.'

'But why not?'

'Kaya', said the woman helplessly. For a moment only the sound of the stream filled the air. 'Come here.'

Kaya shifted nearer her, nearer her body odour, where the woman was lying on pine needles in a patch of sun, the mist wafting above the pine trees.

'You know what it is to want someone, Kaya?' She put her arms around Kaya and pulled her on top of herself. Kaya felt she was being smothered in the dark cascade of her hair. 'I'll tell you something,' the woman went on, a gleam in her eyes, hands cupping Kaya's face; 'the first time I saw you, you were on your way to the church with Beeru . . . and I told myself then that I would prevent you from being alone with him again, come what may.'

Kaya felt suffocated in the woman's embrace.

'You don't want Beeru, do you? He's crazy, that boy. He thinks his mother will come back if only I went away. But she's dead — doesn't he understand that? The dead don't come back. My man didn't, nor will she, or anyone else.'

No, no one comes back, not Lama, not Ginny — and then Kaya saw, in the desolate rustling of leaves, that when she went back there would be no home, not the red tin roof, nor anybody.

'Listen, Kaya, are you listening?'

The woman's arms tightened about her. Kaya's laboured, gasping breath burned her throat; her eyes opened, then shut again. Lying there in the woman's arms, she could still see the sky all around, in the grubby light of the wood, the smouldering globe of sun behind the clouds, the sun-tipped pine-needles . . . and the 'foul blood' dripping into her pores from a million needle-points, lapping against her veins, wringing her insides, ensnaring her in its mesh of . . . of happiness? What kind of happiness is this? *Let go of me*, she sobbed. But all this was an illusion. The woman had pulled away some time back, and now stood to one side brushing off the shoots of grass from her lehanga. She stretched and yawned, and bent down to shake Kaya.

'Get up! How long will you keep lying here? Don't you see it's getting dark?'

Seven

It snowed that night, the first snowfall of the winter. Next morning the hills glittered white. Agitated birds flew low over the town, almost scraping the housetops, hopping from one roof to another, frightened by the smoke from chimneys or the slightest noise.

Beeru's bird screeched from its accustomed perch.

A wilted sun, pale, bloodless, appeared over the trees, throwing a ragged light on the valley overlooked by shining snow-clad peaks. Billows of smoke and cloud swathed the town so that, in the raw morning air, it seemed to smoulder.

Crisp russet plane leaves lay scattered in the corners of the veranda until revived by the wind at dusk, when they eddied forth. Rats, hearing the scampering noise made by the leaves, came out of their holes; they waited a little, then advanced stealthily upon their 'prey', only to fall back sheepishly the next moment. Who could have thought those 'creatures' dancing in the darkness were mere dead leaves?

All this was open to Kaya to see — but not Beeru. Beeru's fever persisted. The only person allowed in by Chacha was the stranger doctor. They could both walk in and out at will. Not Kaya.

Kaya could go out, though. She was not permitted to see Beeru, but she could again see all the places they had visited together — the tennis court, the pavilion with the green roof, the graves of the previous owner of the house and his dog, the tall grass upon the graves, the church.

One afternoon she quietly slipped out to the church, beckoned by a false hope that she might still find Beeru there in the dark alcove strung with cobwebs, or hidden behind a pillar to strike fear in the hearts of timber thieves. But no one was there. The mildewed floorboards had split in the middle. Grass grew in the cracks, curled by frost, over which fell the shadows of bats. 'Beeru! Beeru!' she called aloud. Her call returned, echoing eerily in the deserted church. No one, nothing but the echo, returns faithful till the end. . . . Then she caught sight of the pair of white legs, nailed, and the head drooping under the weight of the crown of thorns. The afternoon light seemed to have gathered on that one spot in the church — on the limp suspended body, the bleeding feet. She had seen him before when Beeru showed her round. He had told her that he, that man, had suffered for everyone: he had died on the cross so that others should not suffer.

Kaya gazed at the figure in awe.

She jumped back as something fell with a plop on the floor in front of her. It was a nest dislodged by wind — a handful of straw with a sprig sticking through. It gave off a smell reminiscent of Mrs Joshua's cosy flat peopled by a thousand mysteries . . . and the familiar odour of stale bread and cake. Kaya picked up the nest and walked out. She put it down in the open. The wind scattered the straw.

She looked on. The strong wind had swept down from the snowcapped hills.

I'll walk away, down by those flowers which do not wither even in winter, which hold their heads high, high above the town. Unlike them, I do not belong here; I'll have to go. Soon the house will come into view: Falkland — what a strange name for a house! The Englishman, the author of Falkland and the Passing Times, *now lies in his grave beside his dog's. That day from the Ridge with Bua I peered at the chimney of this house. Bua is now away in a city across the mountains, and I am alone here, outside the church. It seems that the mountains keep a watchful eye on everything. They are watching me now, as they do the church, those flowers, this open stretch . . . as they will the empty space after I've left. After leaving, could I still see myself here, see my absence, from the far side of the mountain? It won't be something new. It has happened in the past when, even as I remained in my room, I wandered out to be with Lama, with Beeru, with Mother, as if I were but dust, or smoke, which nothing could stop. I'd go over without moving an inch from the bed, drawn in at*

*the end of an invisible thread to wind round them as on a spool. But all
that's behind me now: the flight of dust, the tug of thread, the deception.
Now, in this moment, there is only the wind under the decaying, shaky
rafters — and, even as I turn for a last look at the church, it seems I'm
leaving something of myself behind, about which I'll never be able to tell
Lama or Chhote, for it came to me outside those relationships, on its own,
in this place above the town, where there is neither Mother nor Babu or
the safety of home. . . . Even Beeru will never come to know, he in whose
presence it transpired when I was here with him the first time: it revealed
itself to me in the musty darkness of this church, behind the charred
splintered doors, the wind beating against the bare walls: it stuck into the
flesh like a sliver which could not be pulled out: a dazzling flash of a
miracle beyond the familiar realm of pain, it imbued the skin, glowed in
the blood. . . . True, years hence, I'll neither recognize nor understand it
— so perhaps it isn't worth much to salt away, after all. If at all it has a
meaning, it exists only amidst these noisy rafters, here under this roof caving
in; it will make itself scarce when I leave, and with the last piece of wood
of this abandoned structure taken away, no one will even suspect that I'd
been here, once upon a time, with Beeru.*

Clouds collected on the hills, and Kaya started down the path.
Darkness fell as she approached the metalled road. A wind had
again risen. The gate squeaked. She pulled up by the oak, taken
aback at the sight of a rickshaw and some men warming their
hands over a smoking fire. Who could have come at this hour,
she wondered.

A restless breeze rustled in the oak and a branch swung to and
fro across part of the Falkland sign.

Kaya hastened along the uneven path to the house. The clouds
had thickened in the valley below, while a pale sun shone an the
windowpanes ahead.

As she drew near the house she saw someone on the veranda,
half his face in the sun. Her heart raced even as her feet went
dead under her. In another moment she broke into a run, then
stopped as a cloud bore down trailing a dark shadow on the
ground. She let it sweep past. Then that face emerged again —
and Kaya ran on, arms outstretched, a lump in her throat.

*

Babu stood leaning on the trellis, up there in the shadow of the cloud, in sunshine, watching her come bounding up to meet him.

Part Three

Beyond Consolation

One

When I returned home, it seemed that several years had intervened, although I felt much the same as during those winter days when they called me Kaya and I went to Falkland, Chacha's house high above the town. When I returned, the town lay under snow in what people said was the most terrible spell of cold in years. Many old houses had collapsed in the blizzard, but our house survived. It was still there when I visited this hill-station again as a middle-aged woman, after spending half my life in cities in the plains; it was as I remembered it from my childhood — the roof of red tin, the deserted gallery, the staircase that wound down to Mrs Joshua's backyard: nothing much had changed.

But the chestnut tree did not survive that winter. One night a strong wind blew — the forerunner of a snowstorm, and the town was blanketed in a pale haze. I was alone in my room, for Chhote was away with Bua in Meerut. It was then that I heard the crackling, trumpeting sound. I did not heed it, for the hills often resound with all sorts of sounds in a storm. The next morning I saw the branches of the tree lying in a heap across Mangtu's roof, while the trunk still stood firm. I was surprised because the tree had looked quite sturdy despite its age. Mother used to laze under it on winter afternoons. As a small girl I would make straight for the tree when frightened, crying, sure of finding her there . . .

I had no fears now. I was growing up — but Mother had become smaller and frail. That was strangely comforting, for I wouldn't have to witness again what I had seen secretly that night through the window overlooking the gallery. Mother spoke little now and kept mostly to herself. She would seldom send for me, which was all to the good, for when she occasionally did she would survey me from top to toe, look at me severely, drag me to the bathroom, wash my hair with boiling-hot water, scrub every nook and corner of my body, asking again and again, 'Does it happen to you?' I would shake my head, not even trying to feign ignorance of what she meant, for I well remembered the afternoon I'd spent with the woman with the nose-ring at the waterfall. Sometimes I hoped that if something happened now, I wouldn't be sent to the hostel. So, alone in my room, I prayed to Kali Ma for hours on end that if it had to happen it must happen before school started. But while praying I no longer took my clothes off, for it was freezing cold and the snow was piled on the gallery.

Those were empty, snow-bound days. As I walked under Mrs Joshua's trees, even the night sky appeared to be cluttered with white-sleeved branches — and I fled to my room, to be greeted by Chhote's empty bed and Ginny's abandoned collection under the desk. Lama's door banged in the wind as I lay on my bed counting the remaining days of the vacation, suspicious, mistrustful of everyone since the day Babu had called me to his room, when I began feeling how I was slowly entering an age where deceit seemed to stand out from every corner. I clutched at Chhote's empty bed, I clawed and pulled, the sheet rucked up under my hands, Ginny's collection rattled in the wind, the head of the chestnut tree on Mangtu's roof groaned . . . it was amazing how the maimed tree still moaned.

Babu had sent for me on one such bleak, snowy day. Mangtu brought the message that Babu wanted to see me in his room. This was unusual: he hardly ever called Chhote or me to his room. I started to get ready at once. I never missed an opportunity of going to or being with him. Even the afternoon I saw him on the veranda at Falkland on my return from the church I'd been more than ready for him, and gone on straight to my room to collect my things. So many years later, alone on a railway platform or in a waiting room, I still get a feeling — an illusion that refuses to go away — that Babu will soon come up swinging his walking-stick, and that, on seeing him, I will pick up my suitcase to follow him unquestioningly, without a moment's hesitation, without giving a thought to the possibility that he and I may be bound for different places.

Babu was surprised to see me tidied up. 'Are you going out somewhere?' he said, without realizing that I'd got ready just to come to him. The evening sun on the snow filtered through the window, radiating a white glow. 'I've been to Falkland. They miss you Kaya.' He hesitated, his eyes on me. 'Your hostel is near the house — you could go there whenever you like.'

Was this why he'd sent for me — to throw a crumb or two of consolation my way? Did he really think I'd be taken in? I saw through it and kept quiet. I could go anywhere, he said. To their house, or ours. But I was in no hurry, I had no fears, no hope — I'd already lost all three that winter, and I wanted to tell him that. I wanted to tell him, too, that after returning from Falkland, I had come down to earth, my head no longer reeled, that I no longer worried the bone of the past, that, indeed, there was no hurry whatsoever — but he stood at the window looking at the crimson setting sun spread a gory light on the snow-clad hills. As he turned towards me, his eyes had a wet sheen. 'Listen, Kaya', he said. He placed his hand gently on my head, then removed it instantly, as if the tenderness that surged through him had suddenly dissolved into shame. 'Listen,' he began again, 'you've no company here. It'll be better for you there among girls of your age.' He spoke slowly, in the darkening room that winter evening, as though trying to exonerate himself by calling on me to bear witness. He kept his voice low, which was not necessary, for there was no one there who could have overheard.

Today, in another time, I cannot even recollect the evening, much less Babu or that dim room. All I remember is that as I went to bed that night, I had a vision of a white building — the hostel, I supposed — with walls of snow, spotlessly white, a spot melting every year leaving a hole, through which I could crawl out and go back into the familiar world, to be with Mother and Beeru and Chhote until I had to leave again — when the hole would close behind me for another year. . . . The cycle would go on from year to year — it would never end, I thought, even as I tried to get to sleep, somehow certain that when morning came Mother would wake me: 'Get up, Kaya! You won't go anywhere — all that snow you saw was only part of a dream.'

But those sheets, white as snow — and as cold, were no part of a dream. When I think of the snow now, my mind goes back to Mrs Joshua's sheets, although there is no obvious connection between the two. It seems that my memories are layered over each other, so that when I touch one the other emerges. . . . Mrs Joshua's sheets had not been aired for years. In those days 'help' became a catchword in the household. 'We should all help Mrs Joshua', Mangtu would say. He tended the fire in her room where she lay in bed all day. Whenever Mother saw me free, she chided me: 'Why don't you go down to her? She must be so lonely, poor woman.' It struck me that they had almost stopped calling her Mrs Joshua. They spoke of her in whispers, referring to her as 'she' — probably because she had reached a stage where a name did not matter any more, only the body did — bedridden, a shadow of itself. Nevertheless, I did not understand why everyone was suddenly so concerned — even obsessed — with her loneliness when all those years she had lived by herself and nobody had thought much of helping her.

Even earlier, Mrs Joshua seldom ventured out of doors — now she didn't at all. Snow would heap up at the gate, which either Mangtu or I cleared. I often spent the long evenings in her room, not so much to help her as to find myself a protective spot where I could escape for a while. Lolling in an armchair, its leather covering coming off at places, I spent entire afternoons by her bedside while she slept. In the early days she would question me about goings-on at Falkland. I'd dip into my memories for her sake, but her interest soon flagged. She seemed, then, to be listening to some other sounds. Her mind wandering, she asked me about things that had taken place over twenty years ago when I wasn't even born. My ignorance did not surprise or dishearten her. She looked quite cheerful . . . only once — it was the day after the night when the chestnut tree crashed down in the storm — did I see a shadow cloud her face. By some coincidence Mrs Joshua's letter-box also disappeared the same night.

We looked in vain for it everywhere, high and low. 'How could such a large letter-box just vanish?' she asked me again and again. 'There was a strong wind last night, Mrs Joshua', I reminded her. 'Even the chestnut tree fell — its tangled branches are lying even now on Mangtu's roof.' But she was no longer interested in trees, not even those she had herself planted with such care when she first came to live here. It was end-February, and Mrs Joshua's trees had started putting out new leaves. I raised her pillow and sat her up against it. She looked vacantly out of the window, her gaze skimming the young leaves without recognition or curiosity. It was terrifying. I thought of a hapless passenger who fails to board a moving train despite a chase and helping hands urging her on. Mrs Joshua was that defeated passenger, receding, slipping into the darkness as the train pulled out, even as I strained to hold on to her.

Mrs Joshua opened her eyes.

'Are you there, Kaya?'

'I'm here, Mrs Joshua. Do you need anything?'

Mrs Joshua cast about her as though trying to locate the source of her unease. She seemed to have forgotten that the discomfort of a full bladder could be met by relieving herself in the toilet. When I led her there she marvelled that her torture had resulted from such a simple bodily need, so humble and innocuous, so easy to dispose of.

I waited at the door while Mrs Joshua was in the bathroom. In earlier times both Chhote and I found it difficult, even impossible, to imagine that Mrs Joshua — an English woman — had to use a commode, as we Indians did: the very thought of it seemed vulgar and forbidden. But it seemed quite natural to me now. It did not bother me any more that I stood by the door through which I could hear everything that Mrs Joshua did. Her illness had reduced her to a commonplace body and its everyday demands. Lying in her baggy skirt on a crumpled sheet, the room smelling of sweat and urine and powder, she looked as helpless as anybody in her position would be. Still, there remained a difference, unstated but lingering, which I didn't quite grasp then. When I think of it now, it seems to me that the difference arose from Mrs Joshua's self-contained life: her world had a secure centre, it was familiar and safe, solitary but complete. Its warmth enveloped me as soon as I went to see her, and I forgot everything else.

Mrs Joshua lay with her eyes closed, her chest rose and fell evenly, darkness gathered on the mountains beyond the window. . . . I rose from the chair to leave, assuming she'd gone to sleep. At the sound of my feet, she opened her eyes: 'Are you going, Kaya?'

'I thought you were sleeping.'

'No, I wasn't.'

I looked at her. Where had she been so long, if not asleep? Where did she repeatedly drift off, where did she come back from?

When I went to her room one evening I found her bed empty. She was sitting at her desk, cluttered with papers, the drawers pulled out. The light from a lamp fell on her white hair, the long angular face in profile, the thin body — on which her skirt hung as on a reed. One hand lay absent-mindedly in a drawer, the other dangled by the side of the chair. A ghostly glow, bleached by the snow, crouched in the room.

As I lingered inside the door it seemed I'd seen it all before. My mind went back to the day I was looking for Beeru below the church, when suddenly the thought of Mrs Joshua sitting by herself in her room came to mind.

She was now sitting alone, and I was watching her. Was the face she wore now real? What brings on the real face: the present moment or an earlier moment — when I suspected that something was going to happen? The brumous afternoon, the scruffy snow, Mrs Joshua on her chair — I was sure I was seeing it all a second time round. Things have a way of re-enacting themselves, it is in the moment of re-enactment that memory realizes itself: it then comes to life, turns into a witness and says, yes, it's all true — it happened; it's true you went into Mrs Joshua's room one winter afternoon, and there she was, her hand hanging by her side, at the desk strewn with old letters, the faded yellowing photographs, the theatre and concert programmes.

Mrs Joshua sensed me behind her and glanced round — a little flustered, as if caught stealing something.

'Have you just come in?'

'Yes, Mrs Joshua. Shall I switch on the main light?'

'This lamp will do. Could you open the window a little? It's very hot today. I fell asleep in the afternoon. When I awoke I couldn't make out in the dark whether it was late evening or early morning!'

I opened the window. A light breeze tripped in. The papers on the desk fluttered in the draught. Outside, the February night was very quiet and clear, unclouded by mist. Mrs Joshua's trees stood sharply silhouetted, sniffing the approaching fragrance of spring in the air.

'I had a dream, Kaya', said Mrs Joshua looking up, her eyes unfocused, trying hard to remember.

'What kind of dream?' To me it seemed unlikely that anyone could dream sitting on a chair with the light on.

'A very strange dream . . . I saw I was writing a long letter, but I didn't know how to end it. I worked on it again and again.'

The light fell full on her face as she looked towards me, her eyes rounded in amazement.

'Years ago I'd written a letter', she continued. 'I was at it today again in my dream — but I couldn't recall the end.'

What was Mrs Joshua talking about? What did she want to say? She had never told us about her past, nor had we given it a thought.

Her body started trembling, sweat broke out on her forehead. I took her hand. 'Would you like to lie down, Mrs Joshua?'

She raised her head, despair in her crumbling face — and stood up like an obedient girl. She then lay on her bed and I pulled the quilt over her. When I touched her body, it seemed her bones were burning her withered flesh, and her joints crackled.

'You aren't getting late, are you Kaya?'

'Why, Mrs Joshua — we've the whole night before us.'

'Has Chhote gone up?'

'Chhote?' I stared at her, surprised. 'He's in Meerut these days, Mrs Joshua.'

'Then it's all right.' She sighed. 'Either you or your brother must remain upstairs.'

She was raving, it seemed. She'd let go. She was being borne away before my eyes even as she lay in her room.

'Who's screaming?'

'No one, Mrs Joshua. There's no one here except me.'

'You screamed — is that what you're saying?'

'Mrs Joshua! How can you?'

'What, me?'

Mrs Joshua frowned. Eyes closed, she pulled a face, as if she'd bitten into something bitter. But the moment passed: the wave of pain sweeping through her retreated, spent and exhausted.... She turned her eyes on me.

'Where were you all this while?'

'I've been here beside you all along, Mrs Joshua.'

'Did anybody come in?'

'Nobody came — only the two of us are here.'

'But those people?'

'What people?'

'People, what else.'

Mrs Joshua removed her glasses, looking askance at me. I'd never seen her without glasses before. In the pale light from the window, her naked eyes looked curiously helpless and hard at the same time.

'Kaya,' she held me in her gaze, 'did you get the cake I sent for you?'

'Yes, I did.' I turned my face away.

'Did you eat it?'

I couldn't look her in the eye for shame: if only I'd known better, I wouldn't have thrown it into the drain. But during those long, endless winter days I was not myself. Withdrawn and selfish, I thought of no one else. But that evening in Mrs Joshua's room I felt I must go beyond myself, to try pulling her back from the brink, although at that time I hadn't the faintest notion of how to go about it.

I squeezed her hand. She let it rest in mine — unlike on other days.

'Listen, Kaya. Can you do me a favour?'

'What is it, Mrs Joshua?' I asked apprehensively.

'Please take out the sheets from the almirah — they are on the top shelf.'

'What will you do with the sheets?' I was afraid she was wandering off again, but her eyes were steady, her face calm.

'It feels so unclean — I'd like to change the sheets in the morning.'

I sat there assailed by misgivings. At last I rose, put on the main light, and climbed on to a stool to open the almirah. The soiled clothes lay in a heap at the bottom, below several coats I'd not seen before draped on hangers — all looking rather lost. I gazed up at the pile of neatly folded sheets, white and icy with the accumulated cold of many winters.

I picked up the pile, and put it on the side table. Mrs Joshua sat up in bed. 'Here, let me see — I hope they're not spoiled.'

I placed the bundle of sheets before her. She touched them tentatively, caressingly, a secret smile on her lips.

'I bought these in Delhi', she said slowly, in a distant voice, as if talking of things other than mere sheets, which only provided a pretext.

'Did you live in Delhi, Mrs Joshua?'

'Of course!' She looked up, slightly hurt. 'I used to live there first, I came here much later. I bought all these things in Delhi.'

Mrs Joshua looked around, her gaze lingering for a while on all her things — the gramophone, the stack of old records, the suitcases on top of the almirah, which looked as though they had not been touched for ages. Her steel trunks and suitcases and bundles were unopened, like the baggage of some people in transit lodgings.

'Should I change the sheets now, Mrs Joshua?'

'Not now — I'll do it in the morning.' She lay back, exhausted. 'Could you put them back on the table for the night?'

She took out a hand from under the quilt and placed it on my knees. How white, how thin and bony it was, warm, damp, tattooed with blue veins.

'Which month is this, Kaya?'

'It's February.'

She was gazing out of the window.

'In March,' she said, 'the snow will thaw, and your school will reopen.'

Should I tell her they were sending me away to the hostel? But I kept mum: my unhappiness was too petty a matter to bother her with. It struck me that I was still trying to cling to her, while she was cutting herself off from everyone.

Mrs Joshua lay still, eyes closed, as if indeed waiting for the snow to melt. There were no sounds from above — but suddenly the startled screech of a bird flitting from tree to tree burst forth like a dark shadow on the wall behind Mrs Joshua.

As I went out, I stopped at the door for a last look. Mrs Joshua was sleeping peacefully, oblivious of the rugged night sounds of the forest. Her eyelids were drawn smoothly over the bulge of her eyeballs — and there, watching her, everything came to a standstill within me, as on those other quiet nights when Beeru played his piano, and I felt that something strange and outside our world was about to happen: I could feel it in the air, I remembered it hovering in the afternoon sun over the deserted path down the forested hill, it hovered in the web of moonlight beyond the veranda where I once stood beside Chacha looking at the tennis court below — and now, too, it hovered in the room, while Mrs Joshua slept soundly, heedlessly . . .

I slept deeply that night. Next morning I woke up late — to the sight of sun-splashed hills and a clear sky. The house was quiet; no one was at home. I walked out on to the veranda.

And then I saw them — Mother, Mangtu, Babu, the neighbours — gathered in front of Mrs Joshua's rooms. So many years later I still see them standing in knots under the trees while the dogs howled near by.

I came downstairs, but I didn't get to know for a while that Mrs Joshua was dead. I couldn't believe that anyone could die on a day so bright, when the sky was such a deep blue.

Babu slouched beside Mother on the veranda. Mangtu led me inside by my hand — on tiptoe, as if the slightest noise would disturb Mrs Joshua.

She appeared fast asleep, as I had left her the night before. It was shocking to think that the Mrs Joshua who seemed asleep in bed was in fact a dead Mrs Joshua: she still looked calm and composed. Her photographs, her letters, still lay under the reading lamp on the desk, and those sheets, untouched, white, snow-cold, still occupied the side table. There was a slight difference, though: one of her hands was raised on a bent elbow, as if she had tried to get up in the middle of night to call for help: she was gone now, but the sign of her hand still stayed on the air.

'Mrs Joshua! Mrs Joshua!' I screamed, rushing towards the bed.

Mangtu dragged me away. Tears in my eyes, I stared sightlessly at people talking in hushed tones, the rustling trees, the clear sky. What were those people doing here? What was I doing here? Soon just the dogs remained, growling and yelping on the empty veranda.

I went down the slope. It was a bright day. The snow had thawed into sparkling puddles under the trees. I wanted to get as far away from home as I could. I walked along the railway line towards the tunnel, which stood out rain-scoured in the clear air. There were bushes on either side, and mud, and the slush of melted snow which ran in several rivulets away towards the open fields.

I didn't quite know how I'd got to the tunnel. It was February then, when the new grass sprouts. Goats bleated in the fields below. The bushes around were all familiar. But everyone had gone — Lama had chosen her way. Mrs Joshua too had found hers. Why then was I still clinging to something? What was I waiting for? I'd longed for release from fear, from the terror of others — but this February afternoon by the tunnel I realized that I was a burden on myself, that until I got rid of this other self I'd drag my dead weight around behind myself. This restlessness, this fear, this agony — this thing that Lama called 'soul', that I'd once seen staring out from Ginny's pleading eyes, had taken over my slight, spare body: it whipped around panting, roaring, like a wild animal in the cramped cage of my body in a bid to escape. Sooner or later, I told myself, I must throw myself open to set it free, I could no longer bear its burden, I could no longer satisfy its hunger with crumbs of consolation: it wanted to go out, and I would let it out — so greedy, so selfish, I would yet let it have the freedom I'd craved for myself.

I drew a breath — my first, it seemed, in the vastness of newly opened skies, then another. . . . Then I heard that sound debouch from the mouth of the tunnel. It must be the train from Summer Hill, bound for Kalka. Birds started from the bushes in a swirling mass and veered away along the railway track. The air resounded — but not with equivocation, doubts, or evil: a clean, unsullied sound, it encompassed the forest, and bore a curious call that overcomes pain and challenges fear. I started down. *I'd always stood aloof from the thick of things. Lama never trusted me: 'You only play safe', she would scoff. The train thundered close, and I climbed down the bank: I could yet leave the fringes and stand squarely between the tracks. The afternoon sun shone on the tracks, which seemed clean and pure. I felt I could rely on them, that I could pass their reassurance on to Beeru. There was God there — and in God's presence I would yet redeem myself, and be free of the sins that cling to the cowardly and the selfish. I had been a very frightened creature, but that afternoon I walked on as if in a trance, down by the tunnel where the tall brown grass grew on either side of the tracks. I had no regrets then, felt no pain, sensed nothing. Nothing but a low sky tumultuous with frightened birds, the ground shuddering, the lines hissing darkly, another dark resonance probing, draining the festering soreness within* . . .

The train loomed before me . . . and a searing pain tore through me. My hands reached down to explore between my thighs. Hot, sticky blood flowed through my underwear to stain my dusty knees — it was like the juice of darhu-pomegranate. I thought I heard someone snigger behind the bushes. I fell to the ground to wipe my hands on the grass. Ginny's blood too had been spilled on this grass among these very bushes. At once I moved away from the tunnel, and scrambled up the bank. I broke into a run along the path winding through grass and rock.

When I saw the boulder we used to sit on I stopped. Suddenly I felt light, relieved, cleansed, free. The teeming city within had been overcome for ever, and I was wiping off my blood with the fresh grass of spring and muddy snow. I rolled on the verdant ground. It had happened, I had pushed past God, I had overtaken Him.